THE FAT MAN

THE FAT MAN

· · · · · · · · · · · · · · · · ·

Maurice Gee

SIMON & SCHUSTER BOOKS FOR YOUNG READERS

SIMON & SCHUSTER BOOKS FOR YOUNG READERS
An imprint of Simon & Schuster Children's Publishing Division
1230 Avenue of the Americas, New York, New York 10020
Text copyright © 1994 by Maurice Gee
First published in New Zealand in 1994 by Penguin Books (NZ) Ltd.
First U.S. edition 1997

SIMON & SCHUSTER BOOKS FOR YOUNG READERS
is a trademark of Simon & Schuster.
Book design by Lucille Chomowicz
The text for this book is set in Galliard.
Printed and bound in the United States of America.
10 9 8 7 6 5 4 3 2 1
Library of Congress Cataloging-in-Publication Data
Gee, Maurice.
The fat man / by Maurice Gee.
p.   cm.
Summary: In 1933, Herbert Muskie returns to his rundown hometown of
Loomis, New Zealand, and uses a combination of cunning and psychological
threats to take control of the lives of twelve-year-old Colin Potter and his family as
part of a plan to get even for the mistreatment he suffered as a schoolboy.
ISBN 0-689-81182-9
[1. Criminals-Fiction. 2. Revenge-Fiction. 3. New Zealand-Fiction.]
I. Title.
PZ7.G2578Fat 1997
[Fic]-dc20 96-35044

For Nicholas and Lewis

CONTENTS

CHAPTER 1

Chocolate

Colin Potter was a hungry boy. His mother said he had a hole in his stomach and one day she'd get a needle and thread and sew it up. "Ha, ha," he said. She never let a joke go until she had hammered it to death. And her sayings, most of them to do with food, nearly drove him mad. They were like the holey tea towels she hung on the line to dry and should have been thrown out years ago. "Chew your food thirty-two times, otherwise your stomach won't digest it," she said. Or: "You should wash each swallow down with good fresh water." Colin wanted lemonade and soda. He wanted cake and biscuits and fresh white bread and strawberry jam.

"Hard food for hard times," she said, and gave him a crust with a smear of dripping on it. She sent him to the scullery for some water. "And use the same glass, don't take a new one," she said. Fat chance, he thought. They only had four glasses—four old peanut butter jars—and all of them were dirty already.

They were hard times. They were hungry times. Colin could remember when his father had a job and brought home two pounds ten a week and they had roasts for dinner, with gravy and baked sweet potatoes, and date roll for pudding, and a custard trifle for a treat. Now they had mince stew, and not enough of it, and curly kale, and a spoonful of mashed potato without any butter, and once a week bread pudding to use up the crusts. Of all the puddings in the world, he hated bread pudding most.

He was a skinny boy. As well as being hungry he was greedy, which got him into trouble so bad that he could have ended up in a hole down by the creek. He did end up with a broken arm, but that healed quickly. It took longer for other things to heal—but we must not get ahead of our story, which begins on the day his mother gave him bread and dripping and sent him outside. He ate it, although it was the sort of thing you fed the fowls. There was a bit of meat flavor in the dripping, from Grandma's roast of beef, which they had shared last Sunday. Grandma's was the only place he got a feed these days—meat and gravy, roast potatoes, jelly and blancmange, and a glass of milk. The trouble was, it only happened every two or three weeks. When he went into her place after school—along the old veranda where the beer names still glowed on the windows, although Loomis was a dry town now, and down the hall past the staircase and the empty rooms to the kitchen at the back—she might give him a biscuit or a piece of cake. She might send him to the baker's for the bread and slice him off the crust when he got back.

Colin decided to call on her even though it was school holidays.

He started by way of Flynn's orchard, where the Gravensteins were still not ripe, and the swamp and creek, but he never got there, because he stole a bar of chocolate on the way and Herbert Muskie, who owned it, trapped him and forced him to be an accomplice in his crimes. Herbert Muskie was a burglar, among other things. Ah, those other things—to hear Muskie talk, he had been everywhere and tried everything. But leave him for the moment; we'll get to Herbert Muskie before long.

Colin ran through the orchard, keeping an eye peeled for old Flynn with his shotgun, and climbed the fence at the back and plowed knee-deep through the swamp, around the rushy islands and drowned willows. He followed the rusty creek flowing out of it and slid down the waterfall to the main creek. A track started there, along the bank past the Dally vineyard, where it turned across the swing-bridge into town by the bowling green. Colin meant to go that way and be at his grandma's in ten minutes—but something made him turn up the creek instead of down. He never worked out what it was. Not his old hut up there, hidden in the gully; he'd left that behind last holidays and it was probably full of spiders now. And not the pool, because he had no bathing suit. Anyway, he was too scared of the dark parts of the creek to swim alone.

His mother said, when it was all over, "He had an evil influence, that man. He drew things to him like a magnet," and she held Colin by the arm as though Herbert Muskie might still draw him in that way.

Whatever it was, Colin went up the creek instead of into town. He rock-hopped some of the way and climbed along the bank where the pools were deep. The creek was in a gorge, and the world of streets and houses, and paddocks and cows, was on another level, where sunshine poured down and breezes flapped clothes on the washing line. The wind never blew down here at all, and the air was still. When he heard dogs bark way off in the distance or heard trains whistle on the railway crossing, he sometimes felt there was no way up from the creek.

Was it Herbert Muskie's whistling that drew him to the pool, even though he whistled for himself? Colin heard it, thin and private, before he came around the bend. Then he heard someone blowing through his lips with a rubbery sound. He saw bits of froth drifting on the green slow water. He crept on a little way and put his head around the trunk of a tree and had his first sight of Herbert Muskie, standing waist-deep in the creek.

He was white with soapsuds. They were pasted down his arms and across his shoulders. Froth blossomed in his armpits and stood like whipped cream on top of his head. He soaped his belly and tried to reach his back. Whatever his other faults, Herbert Muskie was clean. He soaped all the creases in his fat and scraped the suds out with his fingernails.

Colin lay under the ferns and watched. He saw the man's behind gleaming like an eel's belly in the water. He saw him roll and submerge and come up with his head as smooth as an egg and the black hair on his chest pasted down like slime. He squirted creek water from his mouth like a drafthorse peeing, and washed around his ears and dug in them, wiggling his finger. When the soap jumped from his hand, he submerged again to pick it up. He put the yellow cake between his teeth, keeping his lips curled to avoid the taste, and swam on his back to the deep part of the pool, where he rolled over like a whale. He was good in the water. He lobbed the soap onto the bank and dived deep and came up with handfuls of creek mud. Floating, he smeared them on his belly and laughed. He could float so well, Colin thought, because he was so fat.

I'd better get out of here, he thought. He saw the man's shirt and shoes and trousers on the bank. He did not want to see him come out with nothing on. Turn your eyes the other way, his mother often said. This was one time when he'd obey. Fat blokes were often bad-tempered, probably because of all the weight they carried around, and this one didn't look as if he'd like being watched, even though he moved in the pool with no weight at all.

Colin crept backward through the grass. He looked up the little gully with the ponga ferns in it and saw the roof of his hut—a sheet of iron jutting from the bank, held with struts of four by two his father had let him have. He wondered if the fat man had found it. Was there time to duck in and see? Even if he came out now, he would take five minutes getting dressed.

Colin went quickly, bending low, weaving in and out of the trunks. When he reached the hut he saw that the man had cleaned it out. Ponga leaves were spread on the ground, with a blanket folded over them and a jacket bunched up as a pillow.

Hey, it's mine, Colin thought, he can't come here without asking me. Then he saw a canvas rucksack at the back, where the sheet of iron was wedged into the bank. He shot a glance at the creek, and listened but heard no sound. The ten-past-two train whistled at the crossing by Ah Lap's. He got down on his knees and crawled over the blanket. The rucksack came out with a tug. It was heavy and made soft clanking sounds. He wondered if there might be money inside. If there was, he could take some for the rent—that would be fair. Sixpence for a night, or maybe a bob. He bared his teeth, half in fright, and turned the rucksack over. The leather straps were soft, the buckles opened with no fuss. A folded shirt lay on top with a pair of woolen socks stuffed in one arm. Colin sniffed them. Clean. And the shirt smelled of soap not sweat and looked as if it had been properly ironed. The man did not seem to be a hobo.

Colin burrowed deeper. He pulled out a razor strop and a razor in a leather pouch, then a bottle of hair oil with the top screwed tight (Colin tried it) and a comb rubberbanded to its side. Why did he need those when he had no hair? And where was the money?

He found a wad of newspaper torn into squares for toilet paper. The last thing, at the bottom, was a rolled-up canvas pouch with tools in it—a screwdriver, a chisel, a spanner, a short hammer with a rubber head, and a midget crowbar only six inches long. Colin knew at once they were burglar's tools and not for a carpenter or plumber. He threw another look at the creek. No sound from there. It was okay to pinch from a burglar, he supposed. There wasn't any money, but he wouldn't mind the crowbar. That would be a good souvenir. Or he could take the whole tool kit and give it to Constable Dreaver, and maybe bring him back and help him catch the man. Colin saw the story in the paper, and all the kids at school crowding around him for once, while he told them how he had tripped the fat burglar up while Constable Dreaver got his handcuffs out. But even telling the police where to go would be enough. Then he noticed a pocket on the front of the rucksack and slid his fingers in and brought out a penny cake of Nestlé milk chocolate in its red wrapper and silver paper.

"Ha," he said out loud. That was rent. Saliva ran in his mouth, and he tore the wrappers open, folded them back, and took a bite. A shiver of delight ran through him at the taste. He hadn't eaten chocolate for months.

The train whistled at the station, far away. Up in the open air the treetops rattled in a breeze. And Herbert Muskie, padding back barefooted from the creek, wearing only his underpants and carrying his shoes and shirt and trousers, stopped at the sight of the boy squatting by his bed with the rucksack open and a cake of chocolate in his hand.

Herbert Muskie loved chocolate. If anything, he was even fonder of it than Colin was. His impulse was to roar and charge. He controlled it. Herbert Muskie was not an impulsive man. He rarely did anything without thinking about it. Rage was running through him at the theft of his chocolate, but he laid his shoes and shirt and trousers softly on the ground. He stepped toward the boy, three steps, and when he saw his head swing around, showed his teeth in what might be taken for a smile.

"Say your prayers, kid," Muskie said, using the voice he had picked up in America.

Colin screeched. He sounded like a frightened rooster. He kicked with his heels to propel himself away. The half-eaten chocolate bar looped into the ferns. His feet slid on the humus, and he went no more than half a yard. He tried to scramble to his feet and run, but the man followed easily. He was round and fat and fast. He was pink and white and quivering, but his hand, coming down on Colin's foot, closed with the strength of a possum trap. Colin screeched again. He thought his anklebones were going to break.

"Shut up," Herbert Muskie said. "And keep still, or I'll belt you."

Colin kept still. He had never seen anyone as terrifying as Herbert Muskie—with his bald white head and black hair hanging beside his ears, and his folded chest and creased sides and blown-up belly. Underpants were pulled up over the curve. He had a long pink mouth with flat lips. It seemed pasted on his face and it ran an extra inch on one side because of a scar in the corner. The scar was smoother than the lips and made him seem to smile lopsidedly, even when he wasn't amused. His eyes were angry. They were small and deep and blacker than sheep pellets. Herbert Muskie was like something that had rushed into the daylight from the back of a cave and was looking at what it had caught. For a moment Colin believed he was going to be killed. Half-eaten chocolate ran down his chin and dripped on his shirt. Then Herbert Muskie reached behind him. Neat and quick, he plucked the Nestlé bar from the fern bed. He dropped Colin's foot, but Colin knew that if he moved, the man would wring his neck like a fowl.

"Like chocolate, do you, kid?" Herbert Muskie asked.

"I'm sorry," Colin tried to say. He tried to explain that it was rent for the hut, but could not get the words out. Creek water oozed in the slanting creases on Herbert Muskie's sides.

"Well, you've had half of it. You'd better eat the rest."

"No—"

"Waste not, want not, my mother used to say."

Colin's mother said that, too, whenever she got the chance. She said it for each crust of bread and scraping of porridge. But the fat man spoke in a way that made Colin want to curl up and hide. He stripped the paper off the chocolate. Colin saw the mark his crooked teeth had made on it.

"I was looking forward to this, kid. This was going to be my pudding tonight."

"I'm sorry—"

"Now I'll have nothing. That's the way it goes, eh?"

"You can—you can have it."

"Hey, it's got your germs on it. I don't want ring-worm, do I? I'll just make it nice and tasty for you." He brought the chocolate close to his mouth and dropped a gob of spit on it. "Okay kid. There you are. Eat it all up."

"No—"

"Come on. It's good for you. No one turns down chocolate."

Colin shook his head and tried to back away. "Fair dinks," he said.

"You don't want my chocolate now?"

"No," Colin whispered.

"I'm sorry, but you got no choice."

"I—I can't."

"Sure you can. Open up."

"No."

The fat man sighed. He stood up and put his bare sole on Colin's ankle, then reached back one-handed to his satchel and found his razor in its leather pouch. He flicked it with his thumb, and the blade opened out. "Your old man got one of these?"

Colin could not speak. He tried, but a croaking sound came from his mouth. His throat seemed full of sawdust.

"I'll bet it's not as sharp as mine," Herbert Muskie said. He slanted the hand that held the chocolate and shaved a wad of black hair from his wrist. He grinned at Colin, lifted the razor to his lips, and blew the hair away. The gob of spit rolled off the chocolate and ran down its own long thread to the ground. "See this," Herbert Muskie said. He tapped the scar on his mouth with the back of his razor. "I got it from a man I pinched something off. Never argue with someone who's holding a knife."

"No."

"So eat up, kid. Be a good boy."

Colin ate the chocolate. Most of the spit was gone, anyhow. It was like eating charcoal. He swallowed and wiped his lips and wondered if he dared to spit himself. He would have drunk water from the creek or from the swamp, to clean his mouth.

"That wasn't hard," the fat man said.

"Can I go now?"

"No, you can't."

"I'm supposed to be at my grandma's."

"Tough luck. What's your name, kid?"

"Colin."

"And?"

"Potter."

"There's a Potter who owns the pub. The pub with no beer."

"That's my grandpa."

The fat man blinked. His tongue came out and wet his lips. "So your old man's Laurie Potter? Good with his dukes?"

"Yes."

"Left hook. Right cross. That Laurie Potter?"

"Yes."

The man was still for a moment. "So who's your ma?"

"Ma?"

"Your old lady. Some local biddy? Before Laurie Potter married her?"

"She was—Poulter."

"Maisie Poulter? Good at sums? Top of the class?"

"I suppose."

"So Pottsie married Poultice, eh? The tough guy gets the pretty girl. I guess it figures." He flicked his razor closed and put it in its pouch.

"Can I go?" Colin said.

"I said no once, I won't say it again. You sit there." He went back to his clothes and brought them to the hut. He rubbed his creases with the towel and pulled on a singlet and shirt and put one leg in his trousers. Colin saw his chance. He rolled away, once over, like a dog, and jumped to his feet and started running, but knew before he'd taken a step that he wouldn't make it.

How could a fat man move so fast? His trousers trailed on one leg as his arm hooked around Colin's chest and lifted him and spun him. His other hand, fat on its back but hard in the palm, caught the boy smack on the side of his head and sent him cartwheeling away into the four by twos at the end of the hut. Colin lay dazed. One side of his face was numb, then it seemed to blow up like a football. A noise like church bells rang in his ears. He felt as if the side of his head had come unstuck and floated away.

"Dumb kid," the fat man said. He lifted his trousers with his toe into the fern bed under the roof, then hooked his finger into the pouch on the front of the ruck-sack. He brought out a scrap of string and took Colin's hands and pulled them, one on each side of a timber strut. Then he tied the thumbs together tight. "There's a trick for you, kid. You can hold a grizzly bear with a piece of string. Now quit your sniveling or I'll belt you again."

Colin tried to be quiet. Sobs rose in his throat, but he choked them off.

"What's that you say?"

"Ner—nothing."

"I don't like sissy kids."

He pulled on his trousers and buckled his belt, which was a dog's head, and sat down and dried between his toes before putting on his socks and shoes. He tied his laces in a double bow. Then he unscrewed the top from his hair oil, tipped some in his palm, and rubbed it in his hair and on the dome of his head until it shone like a basin. He unsnapped his comb and flipped the hair across the top of his head and raked it in neat rows, left to right, down as far as his other ear, which had a piece nicked off the top. Strips of shiny scalp showed through. There was more scalp than hair.

"How's that, kid? Nice and straight?"

Colin's thumbs had swollen and turned the color of plums. They had started throbbing, and his face where the fat man had hit him was throbbing, too. "Yes," he said, trying to keep the sobs out of his voice.

"A man's got to keep himself clean and tidy. My mother taught me that. I hope Maisie Poultice teaches you. Clean fingernails? Brush your teeth? That sort of thing?"

"Yes, she does."

"What's the matter, kid?"

"My thumbs are hurting."

"Let's see. Yeah. You know what will happen? They'll start going bad and they'll drop off."

Tears ran on Colin's face. "Please," he said, "untie me."

The fat man smiled. He winked. "Okay, kid. I like 'please.' You gotta learn these things. Life's a school of hard knocks, they say.' He took his razor from the pouch and laid its sharp edge on the string, and just the weight of it, it seemed, parted the thread.

"What do you say?"

"Thank you," Colin whispered.

"Okay. Now sit there while I think what to do."

Colin did not like the sound of that. All he wanted was to go home. His face hurt and his thumbs hurt, but inside he ached even more at the way he had caved in to the man. He wanted to go into his room and close the door and pull the curtains shut and get into his bed and never come out. He knew he would never feel brave again. All his father's talk of standing up to people and punching clean was nonsense when someone was bigger and faster than you; when he could look at you and make your skin go cold. . . .

"Don't start blubbering again."

"No. I won't." Tears rolled down his cheeks all the same. They wet the chocolate around his mouth and brought back its taste.

"I don't like kids with dirty faces," the fat man said.

"No, sorry," Colin said. He rubbed it with his sleeve.

"You're making it worse."

"I can't help it."

"Waterworks, eh?" He watched Colin a moment. Then he gave a smile that sent the scar by his mouth curling up his cheek. He took his razor strop and hooked it over a nail in the four by two. He held it taut and started stropping his razor. "Always look after your tools, kid. That's a lesson to learn."

"Yes."

"What do you call your teacher at school?"

"Sir."

"So?"

"Yes, sir."

"Okay. Now take that soap and go down to the pool

and wash your face. Then come back here."

Colin did as he was told. He heard the razor slapping on the strop. He knelt by the pool, took water in his hands, splashed it on his face, and washed the chocolate and the tears away. Then he soaped his hands and washed again, stinging his eyes. He had to do exactly what the fat man said. Or else . . . he listened. The razor made its slip-slap sound. Which meant . . . Colin looked across the pool. He could slide in, swim quietly, then up the bank on the other side, across the bottom paddocks of Cottons' farm, and be in the main street, at the police station, in ten minutes. He listened. Slap went the strop. The fat man started whistling quietly.

Colin could not go. He could not swim, or climb, or run. His muscles would not work. If he put one foot in the water, somehow the fat man would know, he would reach out . . .

Colin felt more tears slide on his nose. He washed them away. He rinsed his mouth with water and swallowed some. Then he went back to the hut.

The man grinned at him. The scar curled. It was like a worm living in his cheek. "Here," he said, and threw his towel at Colin, "dry your face. And don't go wiping your nose on it. Use this." He handed Colin a square of torn newspaper. Colin blew his nose and crumpled the paper and put it in his pocket. He dried his face.

"Thank you," he said.

The fat man put his razor and strop away. He packed his belongings in his bag. Then he hung the towel to dry from the nail where the strop had been.

"You still owe me, kid."

"Yes."

He took his jacket from the ferns and shook it out and put it on. It made him look even bigger. He took a tie from the pocket and knotted it around his neck. Then he put his hat on, careful not to disarrange his hair, and flicked the back brim up with his fingernail and turned the front one down on an angle. Now he looked like a gangster. Maybe he wanted that. Colin wondered if he had a gun.

"How do I look?"

"Good."

"Always keep your clothes clean, kid. A man gets judged by his clothes. I wouldn't be seen dead with you if we were in town."

"No. I'm sorry."

"Sorry, sir."

"Yes. Sir."

"Okay. Come on."

"Where to?"

"No questions, kid. You and me are going to do a job." The worm in his cheek curled again. "Then, if you do it right, I might let you go home."

CHAPTER 2

Sovereigns

Loomis was a small town in those days. It had a main street, called Station Road because the railway station was built there, and a town hall, a dozen shops, five churches, and a boarding house that had been a pub before the western districts went dry. The Great North Road cut past the town at its eastern edge, running twelve miles to Auckland one way and a hundred miles to Whangarei the other. Mangrove creeks at the head of the harbor divided the farmland into tongues. On the inland side were hills and deep valleys and freshwater creeks like the one where Colin Potter met Herbert Muskie. A few dirt and gravel roads ran into the ranges and down the other side to the black-sand beaches of the west coast.

Colin had never been to the beaches because his father had no car. He did all his swimming in the creeks. He had not been to Auckland more than half a dozen times. Loomis was his world and it had to be big enough for him. He went to school there, he went to the pictures in the town hall (when he could scrounge a few pennies from his mother), and he played football on the town domain, where the concrete cricket pitch was covered with a layer of sawdust for the rugby season. A rugby club working bee brought it in truckloads from Muskie's mill. Colin's father was always part of that, although his playing days were over (and his boxing days). Clyde Muskie let them use his truck and sometimes put half a dozen bottles of beer in the cab. He tried to be popular, Clyde Muskie, but nobody liked him very much.

The Muskies had been an important family once, but nobody was important now, not in Loomis. Most people were broke, and most of the men were on relief. Shops were boarded up in Station Road. Mrs. Muskie owned most of them, but now she only got rent from the grocer and the butcher. The only one of her businesses still going was the sawmill, and that was on its last legs, not only because times were bad but because Clyde Muskie ran it and he, the local men said, couldn't run water from a tap.

There had been eight Muskies once, now there were two. There had been Mr. and Mrs., he a little weaselly man, sharp and bald and as mean as mud, and she big and muscly, not fat but heavy and slow, and red in the face and wheezy in her breath, and even meaner than the man she called "my hubby." She counted the shillings in her purse, letting no one see, and gave a little squeaky sob as she squeezed them out. She looked unhealthy, Mrs. Muskie, as though she would drop dead one day in the street, but he was the one who dropped, and not in the street, in his office, with invoices looping from his hands as he fell; and she was still alive, wheezing harder, and fat not muscly now, and still sniffing at the coins in her purse.

She and Clyde were the Muskies left. The four

daughters—Olive, Constance, Dora, Maude—were married and gone. They didn't come to Loomis to see their mother, and who could blame them? And the youngest child, the boy, he was gone too, no one knew where. It was thirteen years since anyone had seen him. Nobody remembered him much, except that he was fat. He used his fat, the returned men said, to get out of the army. He didn't show his face in Loomis after the men came home from the war.

Mrs. Muskie lived in Millbrook Road, in the only two-story house ever built in Loomis. She lived alone, in one room and the kitchen, although there were twelve rooms in the house. She was too old and unwell to keep the garden tidy, or scrub and clean, but she wouldn't hire a man to cut the grass or a woman for the washing and the ironing. Some people said she was too tightfisted; others that she didn't have any money left. No one knew how she managed; but her clothes smelled of mold and her shoes were cracked and her leather gloves were split across the knuckles (she always wore gloves, and always a merry widow hat twenty years out of date, with its felt turned green and its decorations, except for one bunch of dried flowers, lost). You got whiffs of sweat from her when you were close—not that you got close if you could help it. Her false teeth clacked. She took them out as she walked home from the shops and wrapped them in a tattered hanky, one that had belonged to her husband, people said. Nothing of his had ever been thrown out.

She walked to town every day, along Millbrook Road, over the bridge, past the jam factory (closed since the start of the Depression), and past the station to the butcher's and the grocer's for her half-pound of mince, which was the only meat that she could eat (her teeth were for show), and her bread and potatoes and whatever else she needed—a bit of cheese or sugar or soap (not much soap). Only one or two of the other old ladies in Loomis spoke to her, and not for long. Younger people let her go by without a word, except for little kids who followed her now and then, calling her names—Mrs. Mustpee was their favorite—but she took no notice of them, and they gave up before long. There wasn't any fun to be had from her.

So she came and went, into town at half past two every weekday (extra mince on Friday to see her through); a quarter hour of shopping; then up onto the station platform for a ten-minute rest on one of the seats, with her shopping kit, a cut-down sugar sack with sewn-on handles, sitting beside her; and home again when the Auckland train had come in, past Ah Lap's, where she never went in, and past the side street leading to the mill. She never looked at the mill, though she owned it. She paid as little attention to the screeching saws as the screeching kids.

You could set your watch by Mrs. Muskie—if you had a watch.

"What train was that, kid?" the fat man asked.

"What?"

"The train that blew its whistle while you were scarfing chocolate."

"I think," Colin said, "the ten past two."

"You think?"

"I know, is what I mean. Yes, it was."

"Sure about that, eh kid? We don't want no mistakes."

"I'm sure."

"You put me wrong, you see, it's going to make me very unhappy."

"No, sir. Yes, sir. It was the ten past two."

"That means it's time for you and me to take a walk."

"Where to?"

"No questions, kid. Speak when spoken to. Do they still teach that at school?"

"Yes."

"What else?"

"Sir."

"Dumb kid. What else they teach? Sit up straight?"

"Yes."

"And?"

"Sir."

"Jeez, you want me to belt you?"

"Eyes front, fold your arms, everybody quiet," Colin babbled.

"Folded fingers? Left thumb over right?"

"That's Mr. Edgar."

The fat man paused with his rucksack halfway on his back. "So he's still there? Edgar's still there?"

"He's my teacher. In my class."

"Standard six?"

"Five and six."

"I thought they would have pensioned him off by now. He got his strap?"

"White leather," Colin said.

"With a bit of tin between, like in a sandwich?"

"Yes."

"Does it hurt?"

"Yes, like anything."

"I got that strap every day for a year," the fat man said. He looked at his hand. "You want to know why?"

Colin didn't, but he said yes.

"Because I farted. Only, you want to know something, it wasn't me. My old lady brought me up to know better than that. It was really Pottsie and his mates. Silent like. They got real good at it. And old Itchy, he'd say—you still call him Itchy?"

"Yes."

"What would he say, kid? You tell me."

Colin swallowed. "Which boy made an odor?"

"Yeah, that's it." The fat man laughed delightedly. "It's great when things don't change, eh? It makes you feel like home. Old Itchy, if he finds you've got your right thumb over your left, does he still whack it with his ruler?"

"Yes."

The fat man sucked the knuckle of his thumb. "Does he still say, 'Look me in the eye, boy, when I talk to you'?"

"Yes."

"And grabs you by the hair to make you do it."

"Yes."

"And wipes his fingers with his handkerchief after? Yeah? So he doesn't change. Ain't that nice? Loomis doesn't change. Old Pottsie, he'd say, or one of his mates, 'Please, sir, it came from over there, I heard it, sir,' and he'd point at me. I reckon it was a game they played, Itchy and Pottsie, every day. You do that, do you, with the fat boy?"

"We haven't got a fat boy," Colin said.

"What, no fat boy? A school can't get by without a fat boy. I'm disappointed in you, kid."

"It's not my fault," Colin managed to say. He started to cry again.

"That's right, kid, have a cry. I cried, too, every day for a year. Pottsie liked it. Itchy liked it, too. It made them feel good. Good to have a blubber in the class, especially if he's made of blubber, eh? You could be the fat boy; you'd make a good one. What a shame you're skinny like your old man."

"He's not skinny. My dad's not skinny."

"What, he's put some blubber on, has he?"

"If he was here . . ."

The fat man looked at him. "What? Go on, finish it. What do you reckon your old man would do?"

"He was a boxer," Colin snuffled.

"Yeah?"

"He won the Auckland championship, for welterweight."

"Welterweight? Well, ain't that peachy?" the fat man said. "Let's have a nice clean fight and break clean from the clinches. You want to know what I was doing while

Pottsie danced around the ring poking out his left? I drove trucks full of bootleg hooch across the ice from Canada to Detroit. I seen a man—you want to know?—we wrapped chains around his legs and dropped him down a hole in the ice. One night, up there. And I seen a truck go down with its lights still shining, right down to the bottom before they went out. On Lake Eyrie. That coulda been me. I'll tell you, kid, after Loomis school I learned not to cry. So if you think your old man would stand a chance with me, you go home and tell him where I'm at. You want to do that?"

"No," Colin sniffed.

"So you want to keep your old man in one piece? Ain't that nice? I wish I had a young feller like you."

"Can I go?" Colin managed to say.

"No, you can't. We got work to do." The fat man settled his rucksack on his back. His eyes flicked around the hut, making sure everything was tidy. "Okay, come on. You keep in behind. And speak when spoken to from now on, eh, remember your lessons."

"Yes."

"Sir."

"Sir."

They went along the side of the creek, in the fern and bush, the fat man leading. He was twice as wide as Colin, or three times, but he slid through the fronds without a sound, with his gangster hat on his head. He did not look around, but Colin knew that if he tried to sneak away there'd be a tug on the invisible rope that linked them, and the man would turn and pull him in and then . . . he could not think. He could only be terrified. The fat man had come up out of the ground, as though he had been sleeping there, buried for years, waiting for something to wake him—or come up from the deep pools of the creek, dripping slime. . . .

Far away, up in the sun, a woman called her child, but Colin could not make out the name. It was a sound from a world he could not get back to. He was in a nightmare, but the man was real. A car drummed on the wooden bridge joining Dobson Street and Millbrook Road. The bridge was on another level, and no way for Colin to get there.

"Stop here, kid," the fat man said. He lifted a ponga frond with his hand. "See the bridge?"

"Yes."

"Okay. Now keep quiet and watch."

The planks underneath were furred with moss. The piles rose from a sea of undergrowth. But the gray rails looked warm in the sun. Cicadas on the timber droned their song. And the sky was blue above, without a cloud. Colin thought that if they went onto the bridge, he might find the courage to run.

"Here she comes," the fat man said. He let his breath out with a sound that might have been a laugh. "Jeez, that hat."

Mrs. Muskie came onto the bridge. She moved in her beetle crawl, and was as dark as a beetle, too. The cicadas stopped their droning.

"Know who that is?" the fat man asked.

"Yes."

"Who, then?"

"Mrs. Muskie."

"Who's she?"

"An old lady."

"Jeez, kid, you want me to belt you?"

Colin flinched. He expected the blow. "She lives in Millbrook Road. She owns the shops."

"Yeah, go on."

"And the mill. Some people say she's rich, and some say she's got no money left."

"Yeah, they would. Where's she going, kid? I been watching her two days."

"Into town, to do her shopping."

"What's she do, then?"

"She sits at the station."

The fat man turned his head sharply. "Why the station?"

"Waiting, people say."

"What for?"

"I don't know. They say for her son, who went away. My mum says it's for her daughters, though, to come and visit."

"Do they?"

"No."

"How long does she sit there."

"Twenty minutes. Till the train comes."

"Auckland train?"

"Yes."

"And no daughters on it. That figures. What does she do?"

"Goes home."

"Yeah. So that was the Swanson train we heard?"

"Yes."

"Okay, kid. You done good. Jeez, look at her."

The old lady crept from the bridge. Her wheezing, which had scratched more softly than the cicadas' song, faded away. Her mildewed hat sank below the cutting.

"Right, kid, you and me are going to pay a visit," the fat man said.

"Where?"

"This Mrs. Muskie, she lives in the house with the two stories, right?"

"Yes."

"So lead on. You're the leader."

The bridge, Colin thought, I can get on the bridge. But when he turned away from the creek and started to climb, the fat man took him hard by the shoulder. "Hey, no, kid, none of that. We stay down here by the water."

"There's no path."

"We don't need no path, you and me."

He made Colin break through the ferns and scrape among the blackberry, which he, coming behind, trampled flat. They went out of the sunlight, under the bridge. No car went over. For fifty yards they kept to the same bank, then crossed on rocks that stood above the water. The bank on the other side rose straight, with black old trees leaning from the top. They hung on to the roots and swung and stepped, and Colin thought that here . . . but no, the fat man was too quick; he went from root to root as smoothly as Tarzan, although there must be eighteen stone of him to swing along.

"Back across that log," he said, pointing at a dead tree lying on the water. Colin went first, without the nimbleness he usually had, and halfway across a layer of rotten bark sheered under his foot and he gave a screech and fell sideways into the water. Even before he started coming up he felt the fat man's hand twist in his hair. It jerked him hard against the log.

"You do that on purpose, kid?"

"No, no, sir. I slipped. You're hurting me."

"If I thought you did—"

"No."

"There's big eels down there. They'll have your foot off with a single bite. And your willy. I think I see one."

"No." Colin curled his legs and tried to climb the slippery trunk. The fat man squatted grinning, but in a moment shifted his grip and pulled him out one-handed. He held him on the log until he had his balance.

"Well, a kid with no feet is no good to me. Be a bit more careful now, okay?"

"Yes," Colin chattered. He crossed the rest of the log and jumped onto the bank and stood there dripping, in a daze. The fat man followed, then pushed him along. They came to a bend in the creek, with a deep pool held in the curve, and the fat man said suddenly, "See, a water rat." The animal's head moved quickly on the surface, with a V of ripples widening behind. "Blam!" the fat man said, pointing his finger. "Gotcha, rat. You ever fire a gun, kid?"

"No, sir."

"They're good things to keep away from. Plenty of other ways to do a job. Now, you show me, where's this old dame live?"

"Up there," Colin said, "around the corner."

"Backs onto the creek, eh? Slopes down from the garden?"

"Yes."

"So that's the way we go. Lead on, kid."

As they approached, Colin saw rusty cans, rotten planks, scraps of cloth, and worn-out shoes lying on the bank and in the water. There was a lidless suitcase, sheets of iron, a meat safe with the wire mesh torn off—all sorts of things. It was like the town dump. But it was, he knew, Mrs. Muskie's dump, built up over the years since her husband had died. Rats had made tracks and burrows in it—under the old window frame, through the broken glass, around the mangle, around the broken cot and the wire mattress. The smell of mold hung over it, with an underlay of rot.

"Jeez," the fat man said. He looked offended. He took out his handkerchief and held it to his nose. "I hate smells, kid. What's the old lady think she's at?"

"It's her rubbish dump." Colin shivered. He was getting cold in his wet clothes.

"She shoulda burned this stuff, not left it here."

"She's too old."

"There shouldn't be old people. They should lie down and die. Go up there, up the side. Jeez, what a stink."

They picked their way around the rubbish and came

to Mrs. Muskie's backyard—or what should have been a yard but was now a jungle. The fat man looked at it with disbelief. "What's going on?"

"She won't pay anyone to tidy it up. That's what everyone says."

A shed, half pulled down by blackberry vines, blocked their way. The door was overgrown, so they squeezed around one side, in a trough between the wall and the scratching vines. Colin, going in front, heard the fat man swear. His hat had been pulled off by a reaching bramble. It made Colin feel better—the man could make mistakes. He waited while he freed the hat and put it on again. "There's the house."

It lay beyond an ocean of thistle that must have been a lawn once. Like the shed, it seemed to lean, but that was because a downpipe had broken from the spouting and hung crazily across the wall.

"Damn, kid, you were going to climb up that," the fat man said.

"What?"

"Now you'll have to go up the tree."

"Tree? Me?"

"Well, I'm not. That branch is too thin."

"Branch?"

"Jeez, kid, what are you, a parrot? That branch by the window. You climb up, you go along, you get in the window. Then you come down the stairs and let me in."

Colin looked at the tree, the bare trunk, the skinny branch. "I don't want to," he said.

"You don't want to?"

"I mean, I can't. I mean, I'll fall."

"What, a kid like you who's real good at stealing chocolate, eh? You telling me you can't climb up a lousy tree?"

"I—I'm no good at climbing."

"Well, now's the time you're going to learn. And don't start blubbering, kid." The fat man rapped his knuckled fist on Colin's wet hair. "Else I'll chuck you in the blackberries there, like Brer Rabbit. And feed you to the eels after that. You hear what I say?"

"Yes."

"Get going, then. I'll give you a lift."

The fat man made a step of his hands and hoisted Colin easily until his fingers touched the lower branches of the tree. Colin pulled himself up. He had been lying when he said he couldn't climb. He could go up the pine trees at the domain until his head stuck out the top, higher than the highest parts of the tree. This one was easy. After the bare trunk the branches made steps, and he went up them until he came to the one that pointed at a partly opened second-story window. It was the only window open in the house. He looked down. The fat man was watching, with his hat pushed back on his head. He did not look so frightening now; he looked round-faced and short. But the worm, the wormlike scar, beside his mouth, shone in the sun suddenly, and all Colin's terror returned. The razor was in the rucksack; the only way to go was along the branch.

He straddled it and lifted himself along until smaller branches blocked his way. He was able to stand and pick his way among them until he came to the wall of the house. Leaves scraped against it, up and down, with Colin's weight. The window was off to one side, but he could reach it by holding on with one hand and stretching with the other.

"It's not wide enough."

"Jeez, what a dumb kid. Open it."

"What if it doesn't—"

"Open it!" The fat man looked for something to throw, and found half a brick lying in the thistles.

"Don't, I'm going," Colin said. He put his hand under the sash and lifted, and it went up so easily, with a whisper more than a squeak, that he nearly lost his balance in the branch. Inside, behind lace curtains gray with dust, he saw a tall black wardrobe and a bed.

"It's her bedroom." He meant that he could not go in. Bedrooms were private, he'd been taught. But the fat man thumped the half-brick on the wall, so he gripped the sill with one hand, then the other, pulled himself across, and dangled outside with his head in the room. He walked his feet up, put his hands on the floor, and scrambled in. For a moment he knelt on the boards, but a call from the fat man, half-shout and half-hiss, brought him to his feet. He put his head back out the window and saw the man down there, foreshortened, with the worm working in his cheek.

"Don't you touch a thing there, kid. Don't you put your thieving hands on a single thing."

"I didn't."

"It's her bedroom, eh?"

"Yes."

There were the bed and wardrobe he had seen, and something that might pass for a dressing table, with half the glass broken out of the mirror and drawers that stuck out like bottom jaws, showing crumpled edges of gray clothes. Dust lay on the floor. Balls of it brushed against his feet as he moved.

"But maybe she doesn't use it anymore."

No one could sleep in that bed. The mattress sagged in the middle so you'd end up like sleeping in a basin. And the headboard leaned over as if it came down like a lid to shut you in.

"She uses it," the fat man said. "Old ladies are creatures of habit, kid. Now go downstairs and open the window and let me in."

"Yes. All right."

Colin licked his lips. He did not want to move from the window, which was his doorway to the outside world. He did not want to go into the dark house behind him and downstairs into what would be like a pit.

"Kid, if you don't shift, I'll put a match to this place and burn you like a bloody Guy Fawkes," the fat man said.

"I'm going."

"Well, go then. Where's me matches?"

Colin pulled his head in and turned to face the room. The door was closed, but a crescent shining in the floorboards showed where it opened. It seemed the only clean thing in the room. He crossed and pulled the door, making it squeak, and for a moment was blinded by light.

Colors shone at him—red, blue, yellow, green—each one like a fire. They came from a long window of colored glass. The sun shining on it filled the center of the house with light.

He drew back, then felt himself drawn forward. It was like stepping into a rainbow. He forgot the fat man and the room behind him. Nothing seemed ugly or frightening for a moment. Then something crashed on the wall outside—it must be the brick—and the fat man yelled, "Kid! You! You play any tricks, I'll wring your neck like you was a chicken."

"I'm coming," Colin cried.

He ran down the stairs, leaving the colored glass—the roses, the lilies, the green hills, the yellow sun—shining at his back. Down at the bottom he was in a pit, all right—black broken furniture, torn wallpaper, bulging scrim. He did not know which way to turn, but pulled a curtain back, raining dust on himself, and saw the fat man framed in the dirty glass. He was from a nightmare and seemed bigger than before. Up, up, he motioned with his hands, and Colin tried to lift the window; then saw that it was fastened with a catch, rusted tight. He called out that he could not do it, and the fat man pointed to the next, so he went there and pulled the curtain back. Dust came down like soot, with cobwebs floating in it.

This catch was easier. He worked at it until it grated around and the window was free. He wobbled it open an inch and the fat man put his fingers in and heaved, shooting it up with a shriek like a run-over dog. He put his leg over the sill and stepped inside; waved his hands to clear the dust; dusted himself. Then he looked around.

"So," he said, "this is it."

"Can I go now?" Colin said.

The fat man smiled at him. Was it a smile? It was like a sneer, a snarl, although it was amused. "Why so anxious, kid? Don't you want to see what she's got?"

"All I want . . ."

"Yeah, all you want?"

"I don't know."

"The kid don't know. The kid is confused. Stick with me, kid, and you'll find out what's what. Where do you reckon the old lady would hide all her loot?"

"In the—I don't know. She hasn't got any, I don't think."

"If she had."

"In the . . ."

"Kitchen? Washhouse? Dining room, maybe?"

"Yes."

The fat man rapped him on the head with his knuckles. "That's where you're wrong. When do burglars come? Except us, ha."

"In the night."

"So where would she keep all her stuff in the night? Her money? Her jewels?"

"I suppose in her bedroom."

"Now you're thinking. Not so dumb. Not so Pottsie, eh? Follow me, kid. And watch what I do, 'cause I'm a pro."

The fat man started up the stairs. The colored light struck him halfway up and made him pause.

"Now ain't that something." He took off his hat. "See that, kid? You never forget a thing like that. The lilies and the roses, eh?"

Colors banded his face. The worm had turned blue. "I reckon you might be in a room, ten thousand miles from home, and not a friend in cooee, eh, and something like this might suddenly come back. It could make you cry, kid, what do you reckon? See that rose in the middle? That's a beauty." The scar turned red as he moved. His eyes turned red. "I'd pinch that if I could and leave her jewels."

"Yes," Colin said.

"But it's too big to fit in me pocket, so I guess I'll leave it where it is." He put his hat back on and climbed to the top of the stairs. "Come on, kid. Enough of the baloney. Let's get our hands on the real stuff."

Colin had left the bedroom door open. Outside the window he saw the green leaves of the tree. The sagging bed, the wardrobe, the dressing table with the broken mirror, were touched with colored light shining through the door. But the room seemed like a lair where something might sleep with its back to the wall, away from the daylight outside. The fat man went in; he felt none of it. He stood in the center, tipped his hat back on his head, and looked at everything with a sneer.

"It beats me how people can live like this. What do you say, kid?"

"Yes."

"I would have said an old lady would be clean. This must've been a nice house once. Look how she's let it go."

"Yes."

"So here we are in her bedroom, eh? Where do you reckon she'd hide her loot?"

"I don't know. Under the bed?"

"You reckon? Take a look for me. I can't get down there."

Colin knelt and peered under. The dust was thick, matted like a carpet. "There's nothing."

"Crawl under, kid. Have a feel. I want to be sure."

He gave him a nudge with his toe. Colin crawled, holding his breath. He went along close to the head of the bed. Rusty broken wires from the wire mattress snagged his shirt. He lay down and slid on his stomach. Dust piled up in front of him like the bow wave of a boat. He found a ha'penny. He found a bobby pin. And a half-sucked toffee cemented to the floor. Nothing else. When he came out the other side—it was a double bed—his front was gray; his clothes were matted with dust.

The fat man laughed. "I'll have to dunk you in the creek again."

"There's nothing there."

"You sure?"

"A ha'penny."

"You can keep that, kid. That's your share. Look in the wardrobe for me."

Shivering, Colin obeyed. Warm, moldy air puffed out when he opened the door. Old dresses, old coats, hung on wooden pegs, old shoes lay on the floor—everything old. He looked in the corners. "Nothing."

"Try the dressing table."

The fat man sat down on a chair by the wall, and Colin did as he was told again. Searched in the drawers, most of which were empty; searched in Mrs. Muskie's bloomers, in her folded stays.

"There's nothing here."

"Well, I'm blowed," the fat man said. "What do we do now, kid?"

Colin said nothing. He did not understand the game. The fat man knew a hiding place, that was obvious, but Colin could not work out what he was meant to do.

"Feel in the bed," the fat man said. "Anything you find you can keep."

Colin put his arm in the gray sheets. He felt under the pillows. Lifted the mattress, looked underneath.

"Nothing," he said.

"So, that's everywhere?"

"Yes."

"Nowhere else in the room to look?"

"No."

The fat man stood up. "You lost your chance to be a rich man, kid." The chair he had been sitting on had a hinged seat. "You seen one of these?"

"No."

"It's a commode. It's where old ladies pee in the night. What do you say? We look in there?"

"I don't know."

"A thing ain't always what it seems to be. You heard of gangsters carrying tommy guns in violin cases?"

Colin did not answer. The man was mad. There was nothing he would find in this old room, or in this house.

Only a ha'penny. Only bobby pins.

"Hey, presto, kid," the fat man said. He lifted the lid. It was like the colored window again. It was red and green and white. Yellow and blue. It was jewels. A chamber pot full to the brim with jewels.

"You thought I was off me rocker, eh, kid?"

"No . . ."

"So what do you think now? You think we're rich?"

"I suppose."

"Well, you're wrong. 'Cause we're not. That stuff in there ain't worth peanuts. It's all glass. But watch me, kid."

He lifted out the jewels in handfuls, piled them on the floor. In the bottom of the chamber pot sat a round pipe-tobacco tin. He lifted it out. Colin saw it was heavy from the way he handled it. He pried the lid off. It made a popping sound—and this time what Colin saw was real: golden coins. Even the fat man held his breath.

"You know what that is, kid?" he said at last.

"It's money."

"Too damn right it's money. It's sovereigns. Made of gold. You ever see one of these before?"

"No."

"It's a pity you didn't look, eh? But we're finders keepers, so it's mine."

He took out a sovereign and weighed it in his palm; then flicked it in the air and caught it overhanded. "How many do you reckon's here? Reckon we should count them?"

"She might come back."

"Yeah, she might." He put the coin back and closed the tin. "A hundred, I reckon. At least. It's my lucky day."

He took off his rucksack and put the money in, still in its tin. Then he stirred the pile of beads and brooches with his foot. "Shall we take that, too? It's worth a couple of bob. Hey, that's real."

He picked up a brooch. "That's not bad. Would you like that for your mother, kid?"

"No."

"You'll stick with your ha'penny, eh? Can't get much chocolate with that."

"I don't care."

"No lip, kid. I haven't decided what to do with you yet." He put the brooch in his pocket, then lifted the jewelry back into the chamber pot, stopping now and then to look at a piece and drop it in his rucksack. When he had finished, he lowered the lid of the commode.

"Okay, we'll get out of here. Old ladies don't need money, eh? Not when they keep it in a potty. Lead on, kid."

They went down the stairs, sinking out of the colored light. The fat man turned for a last look at the glass rose. "Pretty, eh? It's worth coming all the way down from Detroit to see that." But he made no pause, went to the window, ran it up, stepped outside, held the curtains open for Colin, who climbed out.

"Now can I go?"

"The way we came. We don't want anyone to see us."

He closed the window. They went past the tree Colin had climbed, through the path in the blackberry, down the bank by the rubbish dump. A black cat slunk away into the bushes. They crossed the log and went down the creek, under the bridge—no Mrs. Muskie, although she must be on her way home—and came to the pool where Colin had seen the fat man swimming.

"Wash yourself, kid, or your mum won't know you."

Colin washed. He tried to brush the dust off his clothes, but the damp had sucked it in and turned it to dirt.

"I guess you can say you fell over, eh?"

"Yes, all right."

"What you don't say is anything about me. Do you remember my razor, kid?"

"Yes."

"And you know what a razor can do?" He touched the scar in his cheek, making it jump.

"Yes," Colin said.

"So I don't have to tell you, do I, eh? I'll come for you."

"No."

"If you even whisper about me."

"All right."

"'Cause I wasn't here."

"Yes, all right."

"Say it."

"You weren't here."

"You never saw me."

"I never saw you."

"Good boy. This is just to remind you, eh."

He took Colin's arm in two hands and gave a twist. Colin squealed.

"The Chinese burn. Pottsie taught me that at school. And I can do much worse. Believe me, kid?"

"Yes, I do."

"Well, that's good. Now here's your pay." He reached into his pocket and pulled out a shilling.

"No," Colin said, but the fat man smiled.

"Take it, kid." He closed Colin's fingers tightly on it. "That makes you my accomplice. We robbed the old lady's house together. You went in, didn't you, kid, and opened the window for me? Answer me."

"Yes." The fat man waited. "I went in."

"And I've got a shilling for my pay."

"I've got a shilling."

"For my pay."

"For my pay."

"So if I get caught, you get caught. We both go to prison. Now wouldn't that break your mother's heart?"

"Yes," Colin sobbed.

"Okay. Now you can go. Sit up straight, remember. Shoulders back. Run, kid, run."

Colin ran. He went down the creek, up the waterfall, through the rusty swamp. The shilling was locked in his hand. He did not look at it until he had wriggled under Flynn's barbed-wire fence. He wanted to throw it into the apple trees, but did not dare.

After a while he put it in his pocket, where it rattled with the ha'penny.

He ran home.

CHAPTER 3

Memories or Cash?

When people like Herbert Muskie take up residence in your mind, there's nothing you can do to get them out. Time passing may push them back into the shadows, and daily events, happy events, dinners with meat and gravy, football matches at school, lock a door on them for a while. But they're always there, they'll always come out, even when you're sure they've left the district. The most you can do is shrink them a little, perhaps by remembering things supposed to be funny: a bald head with hair pasted on it, a Laurel and Hardy jacket looking ready to burst. But that won't work when you wake in the night and the house is dark and the floors are creaking. Then you remember a razor, perhaps, or a scar like a worm that wriggles in a cheek, or the terrible quickness he can move with—a fat man moving with a dancer's speed. And the strength in his white hands. The darkness in his eye. "Kid" whispers in your ears when you wake at night. It has become a terrible name. "The fat man" is a terrible name.

It might have helped if Colin had known that he was Herbert Muskie. Perhaps, though, it would have made it worse—the man robbing his mother. Sneaking into the house where he had lived as a boy, standing in the colored light from the stained-glass window, going through the jewels in the chamber pot. That could have made him darker and more terrible. Colin might have felt worse, then, about lying to his own mother.

He lied about his dirty clothes. He lied about his swollen cheek, saying he had tripped over crossing the creek. Blame everything on the creek. It was a place where accidents happened, his mother had accepted that long ago. He told her he had found the shilling in the gutter and he tried to give it to her, but she said, "No, Colin, you found it, you keep it," although he saw that she would like to have it. A shilling was quite a lot in 1933 and would have made a difference to her house-keeping. He put it in his money tin along with the ha'penny, but took it out and used it for the movies later on. That meant he did not have to scrounge from her. It spoiled the picture, though, and made him frightened in the dark, as though the fat man might sit down in the seat beside him. There was treasure in the movie, more than Mrs. Muskie's glass jewels, more than the sovereigns, even, but it seemed like nothing you could spend, or that belonged to anyone, and he could not see the fat man bothering with it. And when he forgot him for a moment, because of a fight on the screen, he suddenly saw him in the crowd, just a face that was there and gone, and he spent the rest of the movie waiting for him to come back.

"Was it any good?" his mother asked.

"Too much kissing. Not enough fights."

"I don't know why you always want fights."

"Do New Zealanders ever get in the pictures?"

"How could they?" She was sitting at the table darning socks with wool she had unraveled from an old cardigan. The socks were gray, but the darns were pink. No one from here could get to Hollywood."

"Or Detroit?"

"Is that where they make the motorcars?"

"I don't know. There's a lake there where they drive on the ice."

"Who told you that?"

"No one. I just know."

His mother was no good when it came to information. His father was better. Colin looked out the window and saw him digging in the garden. The clods of earth shone where the spade had sliced them, and his father's forearms gleamed with sweat. He broke some earth with his hands, picked out a worm, and stretched it for a moment like elastic, then planted it back in the soil.

"Did you have a nickname at school?" Colin asked.

"Nickname?" She was surprised.

"Like mine is Pottsie? Like Dad's?"

"I don't believe in nicknames. We gave you a perfectly good name and I don't know why people can't use it."

Colin opened the range door and looked at the embers. "I heard someone say it used to be Poultice."

"Poultice? Who have you been talking to?"

"Grandpa," he lied.

"He shouldn't have told you. A poultice is not very nice."

"So is it true?"

"It may have been. But I won't have people using it now."

"He said you were the prettiest girl in the school."

"Did he now? Well, it's not for me to comment on that."

"And Dad was the tough guy."

He was safe in lying about Grandpa Potter, who forgot things as soon as he said them and was surprised when people reminded him.

"I'll have a talk with Dad," Colin's mother said. (He was her father-in-law, but she called him Dad, and her mother-in-law Mum.) "I won't have him filling your head with rubbish. There's lots of things more important than tough."

No there's not, Colin thought. If I'd been tough, if Dad had been there—but the fat man, stropping his razor, prevented him from finishing that.

"And you forget about Poultice," she said.

"The tough guy gets the pretty girl."

"What's come over you?"

She put her needle down, squeezed her flattened finger into shape. Beneath her disapproval she was pleased. She smoothed the darn in the sock. "He won't look very tough with pink darns."

"He wore red shorts when he boxed."

"Who told you that?"

"He did. Why didn't you go and see him fight?"

"Because I don't approve of men punching each other. Get some wood in, Colin."

"I wish we hadn't sold his cups."

"That's enough. It's done with. Get some wood."

He went out to the woodpile and brought in an armful of split tea-tree, putting it down carefully on the hearth.

"More," she said, unraveling the cardigan, rolling the wool. Her hands moved so fast, they made a blur.

"I hope you won't darn my jersey with that."

"Beggars can't be choosers. There's nothing wrong with pink."

"In a blue jersey," he protested.

"Go," she said, stopping her hands and pointing at the door. He went out to the woodpile again. He wished she wouldn't change all the time, be nice for a minute or two and then get nasty. It was as though she was afraid of letting him see that she loved him. She behaved the same way with his dad, a smile and then a snap, without any reason.

"You can chop some if you like," his father called from the garden.

"You bet." Colin loved splitting the lengths of wood, sending the halves flying one each way. He stood a piece on the block, lined it up, swung the axe. A perfect hit, dead center, equal halves, and the wood shining inside, and the smell like kerosene.

"See that, Dad?"

"Yeah, beauty," his father said, and whacked a clod with the back of his spade.

They worked for a while in silence, splitting wood, turning earth. It was a race, but it didn't matter who won, not like in boxing, where you had to knock someone out.

His father had knocked men out, with a right cross sometimes, or a left hook. He had even knocked a man out in round one.

They often sparred on the lawn, dancing around each other, and his father's hands would flick out and tap Colin on the cheek or jaw. But Colin liked what they were doing now because it was less of a game; he and his father seemed more together. He didn't really like boxing, didn't like getting hurt. Sometimes his father flicked too hard. All the same, he wished his mother hadn't sold the cups.

It had happened when his father was on relief, working in a camp up in the ranges, where they were building a scenic drive. Colin had looked out of his bedroom window in the night, across the dark valley, with here and there a light on a farm, and up to where the hills made a black line on the sky, and sometimes he would see a flicker there and think that maybe it was made by the kerosene lamp in his father's tent.

His father had stayed in the camp for almost three months, until he walked out of it and came back home. Now he followed Muskie's timber truck every morning on his bike, with his tool kit slung on the handlebars, and he got jobs that way, if he could ride fast enough—stacking timber, laboring, maybe framing up. He was doing that still. But in the time he was away, up in the ranges, a man had come around Loomis in an old Dodge sedan, buying up watches, rings, crockery, picture frames, vases, anything really—Mrs. Sargent, next door, had sold the brass knobs off her double bed—and he had seen the cups lined up on the kitchen mantelpiece and offered Mrs. Potter five pounds for them, straight off.

"Oh, no, I couldn't, they're not for sale," Mrs. Potter said, turning a wooden stirring spoon in her hands.

The man smiled. His eyes were slightly crossed. His hat was pushed onto the back of his head. He had a cigarette cupped in his hand and he stepped back and stubbed it on the wall outside the door. He made a little hole with his heel in the parsley bed and dropped the butt in and covered it up, being polite. "I'll go to six," he said. "Six is my top offer. They've only plated those, you know, they're not real silver."

"No, Mum," Colin said.

"Be quiet, Colin."

"They're Dad's boxing cups."

"Ha, ha," said the man, looking at Colin with dislike. "I suppose you want to be a boxer, too? Uppercut." He did a slow-motion one, stopping just an inch from Colin's jaw.

"My dad knocked people out," Colin said.

"Not home, is he? Not home today?"

"Guineas," Mrs. Potter said. "Six guineas."

"Mum, you can't."

"Quiet, son," the man said, "this is business." He stepped over the back step. "I'll have to look at them."

He crossed the kitchen without taking off his hat, and took the cups down one by one, read the name engraved on them, looked underneath. "Not quality stuff, you see. You can see the plating. I reckon your hubby would say take the money if he was home. Memories is okay, but cash . . ." He rubbed his fingers back and forth across his thumb.

"Guineas," Mrs. Potter repeated.

"Ladies shouldn't haggle. Nice ladies like you. Your hubby would take six quid, I'll bet. When's he coming home?"

"Soon," Mrs. Potter said, although he was up in the ranges. "And please take your hat off in my house."

"Sorry, lady, sorry." The man whipped it off. "When I'm doing appraisals, I sort of forget."

"Six guineas."

"No, Mum."

"Colin, be quiet."

"All right," the man said, looking sour. "You're robbing me, though."

"You don't have to take them. But you'd better be quick. I'm expecting him home any minute."

The man flicked his eyes at the door.

"He doesn't like sharks."

"Sharks?" said the man, looking offended. But he didn't argue; he fished a wad of notes from his hip pocket, put a five and a single on the kitchen table—the five so crumpled and greasy, it looked as if it had been used to wipe a frying pan—stacked a half-crown, three shillings, and a sixpence on top, very neat with them and quick. Then he took a folded canvas bag from another pocket, flipped it open, put the boxing cups in one by one. It was so quickly done that Colin could only get out a single wail of protest. His mother gripped his shoulder.

"Now go," she said to the man, "before I call the police."

"Police? Lady, you're loopy." His hat was back on. "I notice one of those cups had a dent, so I'll just . . ." He put out his hand toward the money, but Mrs. Potter brought her spoon down on the back of his hand. He yelped like a dog.

"Go," she said. "Get out before I call the whole street. They'll take you down and roll you in the swamp, that's what you deserve."

The man ran. He ran down the path, the boxing cups clanking in his bag.

Then Mrs. Potter sat down at the table. She pushed the money away and put her head on her arms and cried.

She cried again when Colin's father came home. She said she hadn't sold the medals and the plated belt, they were still in the box in the wardrobe. That didn't console him. His eyes were large and dark, as though he was looking at something he had never seen before that frightened him. They didn't speak a word to each other for the whole Sunday and he didn't kiss her when he left—just plodded away up into the ranges, out of sight.

The whole thing was forgotten now, or never mentioned. The mantelpiece had a pickle jar of flowers sitting on it. The money was all spent, Colin supposed, and all his father had got from it was a secondhand bike to use for riding after the timber truck. He couldn't see that it had made any other difference—they still had bread pudding, when they had pudding at all.

He took another armful of split tea-tree into the

kitchen and stacked it beside the first load on the hearth. He glanced at the mantelpiece. Big hydrangeas there—like the ones growing in Mrs. Muskie's yard. He remembered the fat man snapping one as he went by and flipping it over his shoulder into the blackberries. If it came to a fight, Dad would beat him, Colin thought—but what would happen if the fat man got his razor out?

"What's wrong with you?" his mother asked.

"Nothing."

"Well, don't stand there cross-eyed. Put a piece on."

He obeyed: opened the door, put some tea-tree in. You even thought he might be there behind the stove door. Colin went back outside to put the axe away. He found his father washing the spade under the tap on the tank stand.

"How does just a leather strap make a razor sharp?" Colin asked.

"Don't know. I guess it's the friction," his father said.

"Dad?"

"Yeah?"

"Did you have any kids at school that got bullied a lot?"

"Why? Someone bullying you?"

"No, not me."

"That's why I taught you the old right cross."

"They wouldn't try. I just wondered . . . cross-eyed kids? Kids with flea bites?"

"Ha!"

"Fat kids? You know."

"Anyone can learn to fight," his father said. "What you got to do is punch first."

"And ask questions afterward," Colin grinned.

"That's the ticket. Come on, let's see what she's cooked for tea."

It was mince stew and mashed potatoes and silver beet. And bread pudding, of course. Colin ate his share, and enjoyed it, too, but didn't forget to grumble about the pudding.

"When are we going to Grandma's again?"

"When we're asked," his mother said. "And it's no use asking for more. This has got to do for breakfast, too."

"Aw, Mum." Bread pudding for breakfast was too much.

She cleared the table and started washing the dishes. Colin played Snap with his father. The kitchen was the living room as well, with two bedrooms opening off and the bathroom and the washhouse sharing a lean-to out the back. They played at the kitchen table, which rocked on the uneven floor as they slapped their cards down. Colin could not beat his father, whose hands were too fast. He soon got tired of losing and said, "Let's do gunfights, Dad."

"So you want to run me out of town, eh Sheriff?"

"Sure, Black Jack. This town ain't big enough for you and me."

"Don't say ain't," Mrs. Potter said. "And you know I don't approve of that game, Laurie."

"Just a couple of times, Mum." Colin ran to the washhouse. He felt in her peg box in the dark, sorted out four pegs, and brought them back to the kitchen, where he jammed them together and made six-shooters. He gave one to his father.

"Okay."

They put them in their belts and faced each other across the brown lino of the kitchen, which for Colin became the dusty street of a Western town. He set his legs apart. His father, after a grin at Mrs. Potter, crooked his right hand over his gun.

"So you think you can beat me to the draw, eh Sheriff?"

"Sure can, Black Jack. I got fifteen notches on my gun."

His father turned his head and pretended to spit tobacco juice at the stove.

"Laurie!" Mrs. Potter said.

"Wooman, you jes' shut yore pretty trap. Okay, Sheriff, make yore play."

Colin drew. He always won this game because his father enjoyed falling down dead. On this night he died three times, toppling back on the sofa, then tangling with a chair, and the last time staggering around the kitchen with his hands clasped to his stomach. He grabbed his wife and slid down her body until he was lying at her feet.

"Give me one last kiss, gal. I'm dying."

"Laurie, that's enough," she said, but she couldn't help smiling.

"Bury me deep and don't put no flowers on my grave." His mouth fell open. Then he jumped up. "One more."

"No, Laurie."

"Last time. Promise. It's only a game, Maise. Watch."
He opened the cupboard where the food was kept, took
the tomato sauce bottle, poured some in his hand, put
the bottle back.

"Laurie!"

He closed his hand, hiding the sauce, picked up his
gun, and stuck it in his belt. Faced Colin.

"Okay, Sheriff, you're heading for Boot Hill. I'm
going to drill you clean through the heart."

They drew. Colin fired first, and Black Jack dropped
his gun and clapped his hand to his forehead. Blood ran
down his nose and across his cheek. He fell into the dust
and flung his arms wide.

"Laurie, you fool," Mrs. Potter said.

"Beauty, Dad, beauty. That was the best," Colin cried.

"Get up at once. Just look, it's on your shirt. Now I'll
have to soak it. Oh, Laurie!"

"Sauce comes off."

"And what a waste. We can't afford that."

"Sure we can, if it makes us laugh."

He unbuttoned his shirt one-handed, winking at
Colin, and took it to the washhouse. Mrs. Potter followed. Colin heard them quarreling there; then he heard
them laughing. And when he took the pegs out, they
were kissing. So that was okay. He left the pegs on the
kitchen table.

Later, in bed, he thought of Western movies he had
seen—shot men falling off their horses, men facing each
other in the street and fighting in bars, smashing tables
while the women screamed. The sauce on his father's face

had been exactly like blood. He started drifting off to sleep, with gunfights in his mind, but then someone stepped out softly from behind a horse. It was the fat man. He wasn't wearing Western clothes, but had his black shoes and gray hat on. The scar in his cheek wriggled like a worm.

Colin jerked wide awake. The floor creaked. The room was dark. He was afraid to breathe. In the kitchen he heard the kettle singing on the stove; heard his parents' murmured talk. But here was the fat man, in the room with him. Colin would hear him breathing if the other noises stopped.

Minute after minute he lay still. A breeze came through the window, making the curtains stir. A door slammed far away, in another house. Cats screamed down by the swamp, and suddenly stopped. Still the fat man waited, breathing soft; until, at last, Colin knew that no one was there. He lifted his blankets back and put his feet on the cold floor. He breathed heavily two or three times and no one came. So he went to the door and opened it. His parents looked up, startled, from the table. They were close together, playing Patience, and Colin could see that they nearly had it out.

"Want a drink of water," he mumbled. He ran some in a peanut butter jar and took it to his room, where he put it on the windowsill. Maybe it would help to keep the fat man away.

He got back into bed. Then he got out again and pulled the window down and fixed the catch. He had a sip of water. Not long afterward he went to sleep.

And on that night Herbert Muskie, twelve miles along the road in Auckland, robbed a rich man's house and got clean away. He made enough money selling the jewels to take a rest from burglary for a good long time. He could have set himself up in a little business.

But sadly for Colin, men like Herbert Muskie cannot rest.

The year ended. Christmas came and went, and Colin left standard five behind. For the rest of the summer holiday he did not go near the part of the creek that he knew best but walked down to Cascade Park and did his swimming there. He still took the shortcut through the swamp, but he always hurried past the place where the track forked. The hut, the pool where the fat man had swum, were places that he never wanted to see again. When he had to pass Mrs. Muskie's house, he walked fast. The stained-glass window high in the wall had hardly any color seen from outside—gray-yellow, gray-green—and the rose looked like a cabbage. It was hard to believe it could shine in the way it had.

Mrs. Muskie still made her daily walk to town. Colin waited to hear about the burglary in her house. Surely she'd look in the chamber pot soon. People always played with their jewels and counted their money. Then she would call the police and the whole of Loomis would hear. They might even get some detectives out from Auckland. But none of that happened. She came out of her house, made her walk in her dopey hat, bought her mince, sat on the station, walked home, and locked herself in—never changed. It was spooky. Worse than that, it was sinister. Colin wondered if she had set a trap. He kept away from her and kept away from her part of town.

"Did you know Mrs. Muskie when she was young?" he asked his grandmother. He was sitting in the boarding-house kitchen, eating bread and jam and drinking tea. Upstairs, his grandfather hammered at something—he was always painting, hammering, replacing boards; getting ready, he said, for when good times came back. "And when will that be, Harry?" Grandma asked. "When pigs can fly?" "There's no harm," he said, "no harm . . ." but never got further than that. He went away with a hurt look on his face, but soon took up his hammering again. There wasn't a tap that dripped in Bellevue House (once it had been the Great Western Hotel, but it had changed its name when Loomis went dry) or a door that squeaked or a loose board in the floor. "Leave him alone, he's happy," Maisie Potter said. Like her mother-in-law, she did not believe good times would ever come back.

"Did you?" Colin asked. "Before she got loony the way she is?"

"I wouldn't say loony. She's had a hard life."

"But she's rich."

"Who said that?"

"She keeps all her money in her house. People say."

"Do they now? And have these people ever laid eyes on all this money?"

"Well, no," Colin said, although he longed to say, "I have. Lots of gold sovereigns." Instead he said, "What if she got robbed?"

"Robbed of what? She's poor just like everyone else. Have you finished your tea? Give me your cup." She took it to the sink. "Why do you want to know about her, anyway?"

"No reason."

"You and your friends haven't been pestering her?"

"No. 'Course not. I just sort of see her now and then, crossing the bridge. In her hat."

"Ah, that hat." Colin's grandma smiled. (She didn't smile much.) "I remember it when it was new—it must have been that one. She wore it to the Empire Day picnic at Cascade Park. With all her daughters around her, pretty girls. And that son. Herbert, I think. That was the day he nearly drowned."

"Yeah?" Colin said. He buttered another slice of bread.

"He was swimming out in the deep part of the pool and the other boys dived underneath and hung on his legs. Little hooligans. If some of the men hadn't seen . . . they had to pull him out and give him artificial respiration. Poor Mrs. Muskie fell off the bank. They had to pull her out, too. Her hat went floating away down the creek. It was your father who swam after it. That didn't save him from a proper tanning, though."

"Why?"

"For nearly drowning Herbert Muskie. Oh yes, he was in it. In everything. Harry whipped him for that. Cut a willow stick right there, really made him bawl."

"Dad wouldn't bawl."

"Are you saying I'm a liar, young man?"

"No." Colin remembered crying himself when the fat man hit him. "A willow stick hurts." He knew that from his own hidings, although he didn't get many.

"Now take your grandpa a cup of tea," Grandma said, pouring it. "And don't slop any. I don't want to be wiping up."

Colin finished his bread and carried the cup upstairs. He found his grandfather at the end of a corridor, rehanging a door, and he stood watching the old man— he was fifteen years older than his wife and seemed very ancient to Colin—busy with his drill and screwdriver and screws.

"Grandpa."

"In a minute, boy."

The tea went cold. I wish I could get him a new one, Colin thought. He loved his grandpa, with his skinny throat and hairy ears and knotted hands. But if he took the cold cup back downstairs, both of them would get a telling-off. The old man drank it anyway, when he was finished. The door swung beautifully and closed with an oily click. "Now I'll strip that frame down and revarnish it. These bedrooms will be full again one day. Commercial travelers and school inspectors, you wait and see. We got to be ready for that."

"Have you got any boarders now?" Colin asked.

"Had one last week. Had two. Man and his wife passing through. They slept in this bed here. It was them what told me this here door was sticking."

"It must have been fun when it was full."

"Yeah, your grandma cookin' and me in the bar.

Twelve people sometimes, sittin' down for tea. Good times, Colin. They'll come back." He swallowed cold tea, and his bony Adam's apple traveled down his throat beneath the skin and up again.

"This must have been the biggest building in Loomis, except the town hall."

"Still is. I used to come and clear the drains here when they was blocked, before I went in the hotel business. You knew I was a drainlayer, boy?"

"Dad told me."

"Dug half the drains in Loomis, I did. And there's not one in town I haven't unblocked."

"At the Muskies' house?"

"That one, too. Just because they was nobs, didn't mean their drains didn't block."

"Did you ever go in?"

"In the house? No, boy. Don't get past the back door, a drainlayer doesn't. Not in houses like that. And all them girls in frills and frocks lookin' out the windows, high up like, and holdin' their noses. Didn't bother me none. That boy came slimin' around, though, lookin' for what he could find. Fishin' in me tool kit. I give 'im what-for."

"So you didn't see the colored glass?"

"Nope. What colored glass?" He dug sugar from the bottom of his cup and licked his finger. "Better get this back, Colin, or she'll be raising Cain."

"Yes," Colin said. "Good-bye, Gramps." He took the cup back to the kitchen. "Anything else I can do, Grandma?" He was hoping for another piece of bread.

"No, get on home now. And come for dinner on Sunday, tell your mum."

"Lamb, Grandma, lamb? And gravy and mint sauce?"

"Mutton, boy. This isn't Buckingham Palace."

"Gravy, though? Gravy?"

"We'll see. You'll get nothing if you're not out of here in two shakes."

Colin left. He ran home with the invitation. Mutton, gravy, roast potatoes. Pudding. What would pudding be? "What do you reckon, Mum?"

"Bread pudding, probably." She was joking. "Jelly, I suppose, and stewed fruit."

"No. Date roll."

"Don't you ever think of anything but your stomach?"

Colin did. He thought of the fat man, who was always there, sitting like a blowfly high up in the corner of a windowpane. He stayed a lot closer to his parents in those months. He stayed home and read a book instead of going out. He helped his father oil the bike and pump the tires up. On that Sunday when they went to Bellevue House, he hoped that they would ride on the bike, all three of them, his father pedaling, his mother on the bar, and him on the back mudguard with his legs sticking out, the way they'd tried it up and down the road, laughing their heads off. But no, Mrs. Potter said she wasn't doing that, thank you, not on a Sunday. They walked there, down to the creek, over the bridge, back through town past the station and the shops, and past the churches where people in their best clothes were coming out of eleven o'clock service, and up the steps of Bellevue House.

They went past the windows that still had beer names printed on them in gold letters, and through the dining room into the kitchen—and there was Grandma Potter at the stove, basting the mutton; and there was the fat man, too, sitting at the table drinking tea.

He looked at Colin and smiled.

"Well, if it isn't a kid. Hello, kid. You got a name?"

CHAPTER 4

Sunday Dinner at Bellevue House

Colin nearly fainted. The kitchen tipped sideways for a moment. If his father hadn't taken him by the shoulders, he might have fallen over on the floor. He didn't notice that the fat man wasn't interested in him but had switched his smile to Laurie and Maisie. When his father let him go, he held the back of a chair.

The fat man said, "It's a long time, Laurie. Hello, Maisie. Yep, it's me."

"Herbie? Is it Herbie?"

"Sure it is. Not in prime condition, maybe." He touched his scar with pink fingertips. "But it's me, all right. Aren't you going to say welcome home?"

"You've been gone for . . ."

"Thirteen years," the fat man said, "but I'm not superstitious. Nineteen-twenty I left this town and that's the best thing I ever did." He stood up from the table and held out his hand. Colin's father stepped forward and shook it, licking his lips and not knowing where to look.

"So you got married, Laurie? You won the race for Maisie Poulter, eh? Shake hands, Maisie?"

"I don't mind. Hello, Herbie." Like her husband, she didn't know where to look, but she let the fat man shake her hand up and down for a moment.

"It's a long way from Loomis school. And pulling your pigtails, Maisie. And getting the whacks, Laurie, eh? Itchy Edgar's strap, remember that?"

"I remember," Laurie said. "But what are you doing . . . ?"

Grandma Potter had watched the meeting from the stove. Even she, usually sure, seemed uncertain now. "Herbert is staying here for a few days. With Mrs. Muskie and their little girl."

"Ha!" the fat man said, seeing their faces. "She doesn't mean my mother, she means my wife. I got married, too, Laurie. I left it a bit later than you. Took the plunge last week. Bette and Verna will be down soon; they're just getting prettied up. I told them, you don't need to put your war paint on, not for Loomis, but you know women."

"Yes," Laurie said. He did not seem to know what to say.

"And this must be your young shaver? Has he got a name?"

"He's Colin," Mrs. Potter said. "This man is Herbert Muskie, Colin. We were at school . . ." She couldn't manage to say "together" at the end of it.

"Hello, Colin. Pleased to meet you. Are you a scrapper like your old man?"

Colin shook his head. He still held on to the chair, and kept his hold even when his mother sat down on it. He could not make his tongue work, or his head. Muskie? Herbert Muskie? Did that mean he was Mrs. Muskie's son? What about her sovereigns, though? He had robbed his mother. And then the spit, the razor, the scar, and tying his thumbs; and the man standing here now, in his grandma's kitchen, talking to his mother and father like an ordinary person. Colin could not bring these things together. His grandma said, "Don't stare, Colin. It's rude."

"He's prob'ly never seen anyone like me. Is it me scar, kid? Or maybe it's just me manly shape."

"No," Colin whispered.

"Lost your tongue, eh? Here." He pulled something from his pocket. "Like chocolate, do you? Have a bit." It was a Nestlé bar, identical; the same red wrapper, rolled back now.

"Take something when it's offered to you," his grandma said.

"No . . ."

"Take it, Colin," his father said.

He took an end of the chocolate bar and felt the fat man holding the other to make it snap. He remembered the strength in those hands.

"What's the matter with the boy?" his grandma said.

"Say thank you, Colin," his mother said.

"Thank you."

"You're welcome, kid."

"Can I . . ."

"Yes, sit on the steps and eat it," his mother said. "And don't get any on your shirt."

Colin went out, and through the dining room, where the King and Queen hung smiling on the wall, and

Queen Victoria with her red-coated soldiers, and pretty girls in white gowns leaning on Greek columns, looking across a blue lake at a pink sky; and out onto the porch and down the steps. He went around the side of the building and sat in the shade with his back to the wall, trying to think what to do. The fat man was back. He was Mrs. Muskie's son. And the chocolate was a way of telling Colin that they were still accomplices. He's not going to snitch on me, Colin thought. And yet he wanted him to tell and get the whole thing over. Now he had his thumbs tied again. Now the fat man was stropping his razor. Colin felt as if he had been pulled below the surface in one of the deep pools of the creek. He felt the fat man hanging on his legs.

A little while later he had eaten the chocolate. He did not remember putting it in his mouth, and he wanted to spit, but it was too late. He heard his grandmother setting the table in the dining room. He side-crawled under the coal house roof and sat on a pile of folded sacks with his knees drawn up. There was no way he could go inside and sit down at the table with the fat man.

"Colin," his mother called. He made no answer. He heard her clatter down the steps and come around the side of the house. Her head looked into the dark shed and she blinked. "There you are. Why didn't you answer when I called?"

"I feel sick."

"Nonsense. It's that chocolate on an empty stomach."

"I don't want any dinner."

"Stop being silly. Come on at once. My word, young man, you'll be in hot water. I'll send your father after you. And just look at your clothes, coal on your trousers." She took his ear and pulled, then bullied him along in front of her, even though he was taller by half an inch. "If your grandma hadn't done all that cooking, I'd send you home."

"Yes, I'll go. I can go by myself."

"Don't be cheeky. I'm having a good talk with you when we're finished here."

"Mum"—he held his stomach—"I'm sick. I really am."

"Just sit at the table, then, and keep quiet."

She pushed him into the dining room. The others were already at the table—his father, his grandfather, the fat man (Colin could not say Herbert Muskie in his head), and someone new, a woman with yellow curls, painted lips, and blue eyes that looked several sizes too large. She wore a pink frilly blouse and bangles on her wrists and rings on her fingers with fat stones in them, green and white, and probably glass like Mrs. Muskie's. She smiled at Colin. A little flake of powder fell from her cheek. "Hello, who's this?"

"Colin," Mrs. Potter said, "my son. Who's going to have a bit of explaining to do. Look at his trousers. Clean this morning. Just look at them."

"A taste of Itchy Edgar for you," the fat man said, and added, "kid."

"And now he says he's got a stomachache."

"Oh, don't punish him," the woman cried. "I never

hit Verna. Well, maybe just a wee tap if she's gone right over the edge. But love is what children need. Love and understanding."

The fat man laughed. He made a sound like stones rattling in a chute. "That's a good one. Love and understanding. Did you get much of that, Laurie? I seem to remember the old willow stick around your legs."

"Plenty of times," Laurie said.

"Me, too. From the old man. He never hit Clyde, though, or the girls." His face was suddenly ugly as he remembered. Then he laughed again. "I can't remember a day in me life when someone wasn't laying into me. It's different now, though, eh, Bette? Good times is here."

"Good times," Colin's grandpa said, waiting for the roast. He crossed his carving knife and fork like a multiplication sign.

"Your mother was good to you," Grandma Potter said from the door. "I won't hear a word against her."

"What, my old lady?" the fat man said. "How's she?"

"You were her favorite."

"Does she know you're back?" Maisie asked.

"Not yet. I'm going to surprise her. So you'll be doing me a favor if you keep quiet, all of you. What's she like? Still going strong?"

"She walks into town every day," Grandma said.

"In her hat. That's some hat," Grandpa added.

"Mum, the roast," Maisie said. Grandma vanished into the kitchen and came back with the leg-of-mutton on a dish. She brought the roast potatoes, the vegetables, the gravy. Grandpa carved, and the meal got under way.

"Where's your little girl?" Maisie asked Bette. "Isn't she coming down?"

"She will in a little while. She's not feeling well, poor wee lamb. She hasn't really got her strength back yet."

"Has she been sick?"

"The scarlet fever," Bette said, making her eyes big. "Oh, don't be scared, she's not contagious anymore. But she was so ill, wasn't she, Herbert? We thought we'd have to put our wedding off."

"I wasn't having any of that," Herbert Muskie said.

"Herbert didn't want to wait."

"I thought she might get away from me."

"So we had to do without our flower girl. It wasn't a big wedding, anyway."

"Just her and me."

"Oh, Herbert, it wasn't as bad as that."

He grinned at her. The worm curled in his cheek. "It weren't no society wedding, I'll tell you that."

"Did your family go? Clyde and the girls?" Maisie asked.

"Didn't ask 'em. Didn't think they'd come." He put some meat in his mouth. "None of them know I'm here yet. They'll find out when I'm ready." He swallowed, and the tight knot in his tie rode up and down.

"Anyway," Bette said, getting back to her daughter, "she didn't want to come down yet. She's shy."

"Should've made her," Herbert Muskie said.

"She's a pretty thing. Lovely curls," Grandma said.

"Ha!" Herbert Muskie said. "What you don't know—"

"Herbert," Bette cut in.

He let himself be stopped. He winked at Laurie.

"She'll come down and have a wee bite when we've all finished. If that's all right with you, Mrs. Potter?" Bette said.

Grandpa carved second helpings. The fat man took a lot, while Grandma looked anxiously at the joint. He took more potatoes and poured gravy on. Behind him King George V stood with his belly pumped up. Colin had eaten most of his food. He knew that if he didn't, his mother would make a fuss. He forced it down, although his stomach wanted to send it up.

"And what do you do for a living?" Laurie asked. "I heard you'd gone to America."

"Yep, I did. I spent more than ten years in the States."

"Doing what?"

"I was in the liquor trade."

"But I thought they had Prohibition there," Maisie said.

"Like in Loomis," Grandpa said mournfully.

"You can make laws," Herbert Muskie said, "but business goes on. There's always ways. You can't stop a thirsty man when he wants a drink."

"Herbert didn't do anything illegal," Bette said.

"You weren't there, Bette, so button your lip," the fat man said. He picked up her hand and pretended to bite it, but kissed it instead, then laid it down. "That part of me life is no closed book, so ask away."

"You were running booze?" Laurie said. He looked as if he couldn't believe it.

"Bootleg hooch," the fat man said. "Truckloads of it from Canada. We brought it over in boats, too."

"With guns and stuff?"

"Maybe I have said enough." The fat man smiled. "I don't want to scare anyone." He looked at Colin, who looked at his plate.

"Like in the pictures?" Maisie said.

"The pictures don't show half of it. But no more, eh? I better keep me secrets."

"Speakeasies," Grandpa said. He looked around sadly. "We were a proper pub here once."

"I'll tell you what, though, Laurie. Detroit was a great town for fights. I seen some beauties there. Seen Kid Maxey fight Johnny Doakes. Knockout, round thirteen."

"Yeah?"

"You could've done all right in Detroit. Hey, I nearly forgot, I've got something for you." He pushed his chair back and stood up. "Won't be a minute."

He left the room. And Colin, looking after him, knew it was all planned. The fat man did nothing by accident. He even had a suspicion of what he would bring back.

While he was gone, Grandma and Maisie cleared the dirty dishes and brought the pudding in. It was, as Maisie had predicted, stewed fruit and custard—stewed plums. Grandma was serving by the time the fat man came back. Colin heard him treading down the stairs. How could a man as big as that be so light on his feet? He came in beaming. His little pointed teeth winked with light, his cheeks were bunched, and the worm had only its head out. His eyes, though, his dark eyes, had no fun in them.

He lifted the milk jug to one side and put a gladstone bag on the table.

"There you are, Laurie. I thought you'd like to have 'em back, maybe."

Laurie was puzzled. He had gone red. He had no idea what was in the bag and did not want to play the game of opening it.

"Go on."

"What . . . ?"

"Have a look. Here." The fat man flicked the lock undone. He opened the top of the bag like a long-lipped mouth.

Laurie looked in. His face changed. He put in his hand and lifted out one of his cups. Looked at his wife. Pulled out another.

"Not bad, eh?" the fat man said. "It's a present, Laurie. For all the fun we used to have at school."

"Where did you . . . ? This doesn't make sense."

"Sure it does. There's more of them. They're all in there."

Colin was the only one who knew that the fat man was being cruel. He was taking hidden satisfaction. Maisie Potter seemed to have some inkling of it, though.

"Where did you get them?" she asked, suddenly fierce.

"Hey, Maisie . . ."

"Did you send that shark out to buy them from me?"

"Hey, no. Don't misunderstand. I don't know anything about any shark. It's just, there's a bloke I know, a dealer in stuff like this, secondhand goods and knick-knacks and suchlike. We do some business. I saw these cups in his shop and I read the name. From the good of my heart, Maisie, that's what it is." He put his hand there. "I knew Laurie must have hit hard times. We all have, haven't we? Or he wouldn't sell, not his cups. And I just happened to be flush, so I . . ." He spread his hands.

"How much do you want?"

"Maisie, Maisie, it's a gift."

"We can't take it. We can't take it, Laurie."

"No," Laurie said. He looked up from handling the cups and blinked his eyes as though, again, something was too much for him to understand. "I haven't got enough to pay for these."

"Now I'm going to get mad. All this is just for old times' sake. Were we mates, Laurie, or what?"

Laurie blinked at that, too. His face began to color.

"So, okay," the fat man said, "you had a bit of fun with me, you and Donnie Shackley and Bill Briggs, and I had to take it, but that's life, eh? I bear no grudge. It was just high jinks. It was kid stuff." He grinned. He showed his teeth again, and his dark eyes gleamed, and Colin, watching, knew that it was not kid stuff at all, it was adult. Something adult was going on, and the fat man was tying his father by the thumbs.

"Herbert is a softie," Bette said. "So don't say no or he'll be hurt."

"No," Maisie said.

The fat man turned his eyes on her. An ugly light flashed in them, deep down, and was gone.

"You, too, Maisie, back then. You pretty girls don't know how you can make a poor guy suffer. But look't I got now, I got Bette. So no regrets on my side, eh. Go on, take 'em."

"It's charity, that's all. We don't want that."

"Maisie," Grandma protested.

"Keep out of it, Mum."

The fat man walked in a circle, his hands behind his back. He breathed with a tinny whistling sound. Colin saw that he was enjoying himself.

"There isn't any strings. I just spotted them on the shelf and I thought, Laurie Potter, I'll take 'em back."

"We don't doubt—"

"I'll take 'em to where they belong. Laurie, I saw you win that fight, for the big cup there. Auckland champs, 'twenty-one. You knocked out a guy called Scotty Cameron, round two. I was in the hall, you didn't know that. Just a couple of weeks before I left."

"Cameron turned pro. He won lotsa fights," Grandpa said. No one took any notice of him.

"I couldn't just leave it there, sitting on a shelf, could I, Bette?"

"The good of his heart," Bette said.

The fat man took another turn around the room. "Tell you what I'll do, Laurie. Just so's it's not charity. I got a job needs doing. 'Least I will have soon. If you can give me a bit of muscle, we'll call it quits. In your own time, mind. There's no hurry."

No, Dad, no, Colin wanted to say.

"What sort of job?"

"Ah, bit of this, bit of that, laboring, mostly. I can't be sure. Is it a deal?"

"Well . . ."

Grandma had put Colin's pudding in front of him. The plum juice bled into the custard. She put the fat man's plate at his empty chair, and he sat down. He stirred the plums and custard together.

"I'll tell you what else. I'll give your boy a job, too. He's a likely-looking bloke. I've got one or two things he can do." He looked at Colin suddenly and stopped his spoon halfway to his mouth. Blood dripped from it. "On wages, mind. Would you like to earn a shilling, young feller?"

Colin's stomach heaved. He couldn't control it. He shoved his chair back so hard that it fell over, and ran for the door; crossed the veranda, got to the rail, and was sick so violently it splashed into the pansies on the far side of the path. His mother was at his side, holding him. He tried to tell her that he was all right, but his stomach gave another upward heave, as though a boxer had punched it from below. More vomit splashed on the path.

"Poor lamb," Bette's voice said.

"He told me he was sick and I didn't believe him," Maisie said.

"Here's a flannel," Grandma said. "Let me feel his brow. There's no fever. What have you been eating, young fellow?"

"Nothing," Colin managed to say. His mother wiped his face with the damp flannel.

"Bring him in. You can put him in the lounge for a while," Grandma said. "And don't you go sicking up in there. Harry, get some water and wash that away. I'm sorry, Mrs. Muskie, I'm sorry about this."

"Oh, it's no one's fault. And call me Bette."

They took Colin through the dining room, where the fat man was still at the table, helping himself to more plums. He grinned at Colin. "Tough luck, kid." He spat a plum stone neatly into his spoon.

Grandma had opened the door to the lounge. It was a big room, rarely used these days. Beyond locked doors on the other side were the two bars, private and public, where Grandpa wandered from time to time, stroking the beer pulls and the molded panels. Colin had been in there only a couple of times, but he often came into the lounge and picked out notes with his index finger on the piano. Now they sat him in a chair. His mother wiped his face with a clean part of the flannel, and his grandma felt his forehead again. She looked at him suspiciously. "I don't know about you, young feller-me-lad."

"It couldn't be . . . could it?" Maisie said.

"Scarlet fever? Nonsense. He's as cool as a cucumber."

"Call us if you want us, Colin. We're only in the next room."

They left him alone in an easy chair that normally his grandma forbade him to sit in. He lay with the folded flannel on his brow and heard his grandpa hosing the path. He felt no better now that he'd been sick; in fact, he felt worse. His stomach was all right, but his head had too much in it. The fat man was still after him. And after his mother and father, too. The sound of spoons tinkling on plates came from the dining room. His grandpa came back and said, "Done it."

"Wash your hands, Harry," Grandma said.

"Didn't touch nothing. Washed 'em under the hose, anyway."

"I'll eat that young feller's plums," the fat man said. "If no one wants them."

"He's got no bottom to his stomach," Bette said.

"Got to keep me strength up." His voice seemed to come from beside Colin's ear. Colin lifted the flannel and turned his head. He saw the fat man through the open door, spooning up custard. And the fat man saw him, turning by a kind of magnetism. He winked. Colin tried not to be sick again. He managed it. He felt he was unraveling like an old jersey. He covered his eyes with the flannel, but that was little help; the fat man was still there through the open door. Everyone else had finished and was waiting politely His spoon scraped on his plate. At last he sighed. "Ah, that's good. That's as good a feed as I've had in years."

"Cooking was one of the things we was known for in this pub," Grandpa said.

"What we need now . . . you know what we need, Laurie?"

Although he could not see him, Colin felt the fat man grinning at his father. Leave Dad alone, he wanted to say. He heard him push his chair back and leave the table; heard him climb the stairs again. The ceiling creaked over his head and he thought he heard, far off, the sound of a laugh. Then his mother and father and Bette came into the lounge. His mother took the flannel away and studied his face, while Bette said, "Poor lamb," again, which

Colin didn't care for. He smelled her scent and felt a flake of powder from her cheek settle on his nose.

"Can we go soon?" he asked.

"How do you feel?"

"Can we?"

"As soon as we've had a cup of tea."

"Tea!" the fat man cried, coming in. "We're not drinking that stuff, not when all us old friends get together after so long. This is a celebration, Maisie." He showed four bottles of beer, dangling by their necks, two in each hand. Then he shouted back through the door, "Hey, Mrs. Potter, Mr. Potter, cancel that tea. Bring a bottle opener and some glasses and have a beer." He smiled at Laurie. "We could run a sly grog shop from here. Make us a few bob, eh, what do you think?"

"I'd prefer tea, thank you," Maisie said.

"Me, too, Herbert," Bette said. "You know I don't like beer."

"Gives her the wind," the fat man said. "Okay, tea for the ladies, beer for the men. Ah, glasses, Harry. You'll have one, won't you?"

"You bet," Grandpa said. "I might have two."

So the men drank beer while the ladies had tea. Herbert Muskie produced three cigars from a pocket. "Laurie. Harry." They lit up and puffed, sitting in their chairs. Aromatic smoke filled the lounge.

Colin got his flannel back and covered his eyes. He heard the fat man's voice. "You know what I reckon you should have, kid? A beer."

"No," Maisie said sharply.

"No offense. I just thought it might settle his stomach."

"He's too young."

"We started young, eh, Laurie, you and me?"

Colin's father laughed. He sounded easier.

"Let's have some music," the fat man said. He got up and went to the piano, lifted the lid, struck a note. "It works."

"Harry tunes it," Grandma said.

"I got an ear," Grandpa said, "but I don't play. No one plays now."

"Maisie?" the fat man asked.

"I never learned."

"It looks like you then, Bette."

"Oh no, I couldn't."

"Sure you could. Bette used to sing on the stage. Musical comedy. Eh, Bette? Give us a song."

"Well, Herbert, if you insist . . ."

"I do. I insist." He winked at Maisie. "Try and stop her."

Colin lifted his flannel. He saw the woman settle herself on the piano stool. She took off her rings, flexed her fingers, and started to play. To Colin it seemed she played well: a tune tinkled out, with the notes going fast, and no mistakes. In a sweet, tinny voice, she sang, "You're the cream in my coffee . . ."

"Hey, yey," Grandpa cried. The beer seemed to have gone to his head.

Everybody clapped when she had finished. She smiled back over her shoulder and raised a little question mark with her eyebrows at the fat man.

"Yeah, don't stop," he said.

She sang "Life is just a bowl of cherries" and "I'm forever blowing bubbles," her voice like a cracked glass, sharp and frail and a little off-key. Then she sang a slow one, "When I was twenty-one and you were sweet sixteen," which wasn't so good.

Colin had put his flannel on the floor. He risked a look at the fat man. He was lying back in an easy chair with his feet splayed out. His hands were folded on his belly, and his head rested on the back of the chair. The cigar, with an inch of ash, burned in his mouth, sending a plume of smoke at the ceiling. Without moving it, he said, "Happy days are here again." Then he took it out and smiled at Maisie. "My favorite."

Bette sang, "Happy days are here again, The skies are growing clear again . . ."

A movement at the open door caught Colin's eye. A girl was standing there, behind the fat man; a skinny girl with a frown on her face. She wore a pink dress and a pink and white bonnet. Brown curls hung beside her cheeks. Her mouth was twisted as though she tasted something bad. She took a step forward as the people in the room clapped Bette's song. "Mum," she said, and at the same instant the fat man flattened his feet on the floor and straightened his legs. His chair skidded back across the floor. Without even looking, he reached over his head and grabbed the girl by the arms. "Gotcha," he said.

She shrieked and tried to pull away, but he held her fast. His cigar sent smoke into her face. He looked at her upwards and said, "Sneaking in?"

"No, I wasn't. Let me go."

Bette had jumped up from the piano. "Herbert, you're hurting her," she cried.

"No, I'm not. Just giving her a squeeze." But he let her go, and the girl ran to Bette, who took her in her arms.

"There, there, he didn't mean it. He's just a big hooligan."

"Cuddling me daughter, that's all," the fat man said.

"I'm not your daughter," the girl said from her mother's arms.

"You are if I say so," the fat man said. For a moment he looked discomforted, then he laughed. "What do you think of her bonnet, ladies and gents?"

"Herbert," Bette warned.

"And her pretty curls?"

"There, love," Bette said. "Take no notice of him. Are you feeling better?"

"I heard you singing," the girl said.

"I was entertaining the company." She smiled around. "Concert's over. This is Verna, my little girl."

"I'm not little."

"You're sure as hell not big," the fat man said. "You wouldn't think she was twelve, would you? If I really was her dad, she'd have some beef on her."

"Herbert," Bette warned again. Then she said to Verna, "Would you like some dinner, love? Some pudding? Plums and custard?"

"No plums left, I ate 'em all," the fat man said.

"Mrs. Potter kept some, so don't be smart, Herbert," Bette said.

"Sorry, ma'am." He puffed his cigar and tapped the ash into the ashtray Grandma had put on the table at his side.

"I'm not hungry," the girl said.

"Just a little bit? Lovely plums . . . ?"

"I said I'm not hungry."

Colin felt sympathy for Verna—adult eyes all watching her. Her bonnet was a joke, though. Who'd wear that? But he watched her with a horrified interest as well—having the fat man as a father. He could see that she was what people might call pretty—eyes and nose and mouth and curls—even though she was too thin and knobbly for twelve.

The fat man said, "When she goes to school, kid, she'll probably be in your class. Old Itchy can strap the pair of you."

"I'm not going to school," Verna said. "Not here."

"Not yet, anyway," Bette said.

"You'll go where we put you," the fat man said. "But maybe not here. We gotta see if we're welcome yet."

"Sure you're welcome," Grandpa said, pouring more beer in his glass.

"That's enough of that, Harry," Grandma said.

"Hey, let him drink," the fat man said. "Life's too short. All of us might be dead tomorrow."

"What a dreadful thing to say, Herbert," Bette said. She still held her daughter in one arm.

"You reckon it's a bowl of cherries, eh?" He grinned at her, then at Maisie and Laurie. "Well, maybe it is. There might be some nice old gent up there"—prodding with his cigar at the ceiling—"smiling down. But he didn't treat you too well, eh, Vern? Scarlet fever."

"Leave her alone, Herbert," Bette said.

He ignored her. "Come here, girl."

"No."

"Come on, I won't hurt you."

"No." Verna turned her eyes up at her mother. "Mum?"

"Just send her across here, Bette," the fat man said. "There's a coupla things I got to say."

"Herbert . . ."

He smiled at her. "Bette, you're Mrs. Muskie now." His voice had gone softer. The worm in his cheek gave a jerk.

Underneath her powder, Bette turned pale. She swallowed and managed to make a rigid smile. "Go on, love." She gave a tiny push on Verna's shoulders. "Go to your father. You'll be all right."

The girl crossed the space. Her legs carried her like puppet legs. The fat man smiled and laid down his cigar. He had pushed himself upright in his chair and he took her upper arms in his hands. "Vern," he said, "if I say you go to Loomis school, that's where you go. Understand?"

She managed to nod. Her eyes were fixed on him with a glazed look.

"And if I say you eat your plums, you eat."

Again, she nodded.

"Say, 'Yes, Dad.'"

"Yes, Dad." It was so soft, Colin barely heard.

"And if I say you don't wear your bonnet inside, then you don't wear it."

"Herbert," Bette said. She took a step forward, with her hands held like a prayer.

"Stay there, Bette. And keep your trap shut. This is between me and Vern."

He smiled at the girl. He let her arms go.

"So take it off."

Verna trembled, but she obeyed. Her fingers pulled the bow undone beneath her chin. The ribbons fell down, and her arms fell, too, hanging loosely.

"Good girl," the fat man said. "Now, nice and easy, hats off. And keep out of it, Bette," he added as his wife seemed on the point of stepping forward.

"Stop," Maisie Potter said. "You can't . . ." but could not finish. The fat man flicked his eyes at her and gave a smile.

"Things have changed, Maisie. So stay out of it."

A tear slipped from Verna's eye. The fat man put his finger out and squashed it. "No use crying," he said.

Slowly she raised her hands and took her bonnet off. Again her arms fell to her sides. The bonnet ribbons dangled on the floor. But no one was looking at that. Verna's curls were gone. They were sewn into the bonnet. Soft hair, not half an inch long, covered her head. She was shorn like a sheep. Colin thought she still looked all right—like a boy. But Grandma Potter said, "Oh, the poor little thing."

Bette ran forward and caught Verna in her arms. "I hope you're satisfied," she said to the fat man.

"Nope," he said. "I just don't like hats on in the house. My mother taught me it was bad manners."

But Colin saw the pleasure he took from what he'd done. He found the flannel and put it over his eyes. "She better have her plums now," he heard the fat man say. "Lucky there's some left"—and heard Bette take Verna out of the room.

The men smoked their cigars and finished the bottles of beer. Then the Potters went home.

"Why's her hair like that, Mum?" Colin said.

"The scarlet fever."

"Does it make your hair fall out?"

"No, they shave it off. It's part of the treatment."

"That hair sewn in her hat really fooled me," Laurie said.

"I'm not surprised, the amount of beer you were drinking. Laurie, I won't have that man in the house. And I don't want you working for him, either. There's something wrong with him. He was cruel to that girl."

Yes, Dad, Colin wanted to say, keep away from him, he's after us.

But Laurie Potter kept quiet. He carried the gladstone bag. The boxing cups clanked against his knee as they walked through town.

When they got home, he put them in a neat line on the mantelpiece. Then he stood back and admired them.

CHAPTER 5

Green Hair

"You will if I say you will," Mrs. Potter said, and she banged the kettle on the stove and gave the fire a poke.

They had been arguing for half an hour, and Colin had not budged her an inch. He knew she understood why he couldn't do it—walk to school with a new girl, especially when her hair was only half an inch long—but it seemed she didn't care. All she cared about was Verna Muskie.

"The other kids, they'll think . . ." he said. She knew what they would think, but "Let them" was all she said again.

Colin decided he would run away. He'd spend the day in the bush down by Cascade Park. Or else he'd take the train to Auckland and spend the day in there. He had enough for the fare in his money tin.

"All I'm asking," Mrs. Potter said, "is that you call for her at Mum and Dad's and walk to school with her. And take her to the headmaster's office. That's all. Just say to Mr. Garvey, this is Verna Muskie and leave it at that. She'll have a letter from her mother. You don't have to walk home with her after school—although it would be nice if you did."

"The other kids—"

"Colin! I'm not telling you again. Now go and clean your teeth. And make sure your fingernails are clean."

"Why can't her mother take her?" But he knew the answer to that. Because Herbert Muskie said no. The girl had to learn to stand on her own two feet. And she had to leave her hat at home.

What the fat man said, Bette and Verna had to do. He had agreed that Colin would call for her at Bellevue House.

Colin brushed his teeth, using salt, and got his schoolbag from his room. He put his lunch in it and thought, now for Cascade Park. But the trouble there would be and the whipping he would get. It wasn't that which stopped him, though, it was the fat man. If he hid in the bush at the park, or anywhere, the fat man would turn up in his car and hunt him out.

"Kiss," Mrs. Potter said as he went out the door. Colin came back and kissed her cheek.

"I do know how you feel," she said. "But she's lonely and she's frightened and she knows how funny she looks. So just be kind."

He said nothing.

"And she's got Herbert Muskie for a father."

"Yes," Colin said.

He walked through the streets to Bellevue House. He hadn't seen Verna Muskie in the week since they'd gone to dinner, but he knew her hair couldn't have grown much in that time. It would still be as flat as knitting on her head.

He walked past the station and saw Herbert Muskie's car nose out from Bellevue House and turn toward him. It was a Buick, painted dark green, with the headlights and door handles and grille shining silver. Colin had no time to duck into the station. The fat man slowed down and stopped. He sat looking at Colin. Grandpa Potter grinned beside him.

"Morning, kid. How's your stomach now?" the fat man said.

"I'm all right," Colin said.

"You don't need a dose of castor oil?"

"Ha, ha," Grandpa laughed. Colin felt cold and small. He had them, the fat man, he had Colin's father and grandpa eating out of his hand.

"You look after my little girl and I'll have a shilling for you," the fat man said. He winked at Colin. "Chin up, kid." He drove away. The Buick left a haze of blue exhaust in the air.

The fat man had owned it for a week. On the Monday after the Potters' dinner at Bellevue House he had caught the morning train into Auckland, and had turned up again before midday, driving into Station Road and into the boarding house yard. He honked the horn, bringing Bette and Grandma and Grandpa running out. (Verna watched from an upstairs window.) They oohed and aahed at the car, stroked it, tried the horn, and Grandpa, who was good at all mechanical things, looked under the bonnet and rubbed his hands. The fat man took them for a ride through Loomis and then for a mile or two along the Great North Road. He wound the Buick up to sixty miles an hour. And everyone in Loomis knew what had happened later in the day. Some of them had seen it. It was, Mrs. Sargent said, the loveliest thing she'd ever seen, it had made her cry. It went like this:

Herbert Muskie and Grandpa Potter drove out to Sunnyvale Station—just a little hut it was, on the near side of the creek, with Sunnyvale painted over the door— and Herbert Muskie waited there while Grandpa drove the Buick back to Loomis. Mrs. Muskie came into town not long after that, keeping to her timetable—grocer, butcher, station—and when the three o'clock train pulled in from Auckland, she stood up as she always did and watched to see who stepped down from the carriages. When it was Herbert Muskie, grinning, easy, with a cigarette in his mouth and his hat tipped on the back of his head, she let out a shriek. She almost fell over—did a sideways stagger and held herself up against a goods trolley standing there.

Herbert Muskie ground his cigarette out with the toe of his shoe and went up to her and said, "Here I am, Mum. I've come home," and he took her in his arms (Mrs. Sargent wipes her eye) and kissed her so her hat tipped backward at the same angle as his. Then he led her down the ramp to his waiting car and put her in the back seat like the Queen, and Grandpa got out and he got in and drove her through Loomis, across the bridge she'd wheezed over half an hour before, to the two-story falling-down house by the creek.

"What a wonderful son," Mrs. Sargent said.

It's not true, Colin had wanted to yell when he heard

it, can't you see he's fooling everyone. But no one would have listened. They'd all gone loopy over the fat man, they couldn't get enough of him. Later in the day Muskie drove back to Bellevue House and took Bette and Verna to meet his mother. No one knew how that had turned out, but they all had dinner at Bellevue House that night, and Bette sang songs that made the old lady cry. She still lived by herself in the house by the creek. Herbert and his family weren't shifting in until it was done up; they'd stay at Bellevue House until Laurie Potter had finished the repairs. Yes, Laurie was to do it. What good luck for the Potters, getting a job like that when times were so hard.

As for Clyde Muskie, poor old Clyde, Herbert had shaken hands with him and patted him on the shoulder. He had gone to see the sawmill and given Clyde a cigar and left it at that. He had given Laurie Potter another cigar, too, as they looked at what needed doing to Mrs. Muskie's house. Laurie came home with half of it stuck behind his ear for later on.

"No," Maisie Potter said, "I don't want you working for him."

"Ah, come on, Maise, he's not so bad."

"What does he want you to do?"

"Pull the old garden shed down first. I'm doing that for nothing, for my cups. After that he's going to give me one and six an hour. That's good money, Maise."

"For what?"

"Clearing the section."

"You're not a gardener."

"And painting the house."

"You're not a painter."

"There's a lot of carpentry, too. All the doors and windows need unsticking. There's rotten weatherboards. And rusty iron on the roof. She's got buckets everywhere, catching the leaks. He might even want a new flush toilet put in."

Maisie Potter did not say, You're not a plumber. "How long is it going to take?" she said.

"Maybe three months. Three months of good wages, Maise." He took the half-cigar from behind his ear.

"Smoke that outside," Maisie said. "And don't bring Herbert Muskie here." She turned to her cooking. "I don't know where he got his money—"

"America."

"—but I'm sure it wasn't honest."

"He wants Dad to re-lay the drains," Laurie said. "So don't blame only me." He did not like being sent outside.

Maisie damped the fire down. "What does he want? Why is he picking on us?" she asked the stove.

Colin did not know, either. All he knew was that the fat man had got them. And Bette and Verna had got his mother. She was trying to fight Herbert Muskie by being kind to them.

He went into the yard at Bellevue House. No one was around. The Muskies were still the only boarders, and they would be there until the repairs on Mrs. Muskie's house were done. In all ways the Potters were doing well out of the fat man. It was almost as if he'd come back to Loomis to help them out. Monday morning, and Colin's grandma had already pegged Bette and Verna's washing on the line.

Colin stood and waited. He wasn't going in for her. If she doesn't come by the time I count to fifty, he thought . . . But he hadn't got to ten when Bette and Verna came onto the veranda. Colin could not believe the way Verna was dressed: a pink dress, frills, red shoes, white socks. She carried a little brown polished case instead of a schoolbag.

No, he wailed inside himself.

"Colin," Bette Muskie trilled. She smiled at him, but seemed to frown at the same time at his bare feet. "It's nice of you to look after Verna. She's a wee bit nervous, aren't you, pet? It's her hair. Tell them it's the latest fashion from America. No? You tell them, Colin. Don't let them tease my little girl."

They would do more than tease, Colin knew, and not only because of her hair. There were only half a dozen kids at school who wore shoes. "She can have bare feet," he said.

"Oh, good heavens, we haven't sunk to that," Bette replied. "Now kiss me, pet. Mmm. And off you go. You can't be late on your first morning."

Verna came down the steps. She had not looked at Colin. She walked ahead of him out of the yard, with her hair shining in the sun. Her shoes, shining, too, went click clack as she turned into Station Road. Colin looked around. There were no kids in sight. He ran a step and got at her side, but could not think of anything to say.

"You don't have to walk with me," Verna said.

"Sure, if you don't want me to," he said. He ran and got ten yards ahead but could not make himself get further than that. She was like something pinned on him that he could not shake off. He got to the corner of Great North Road, saw none of his schoolmates there, and waited for her.

"You can take your shoes off."

"No," Verna said.

"No one wears shoes. You can walk on anything when you're used to it." He showed her his soles, which were yellow and calloused and cracked. She took no notice of them and walked on.

"Can't you get a wig? For school?" he said.

"He wouldn't let me."

Colin swallowed. He looked over his shoulder, half-expecting the fat man to be there. "What's it like, living with him?"

She made no answer but kept walking on the weedy footpath. Red shoes—click clack. Her face was sharp—sharp upper lip like the prow of a canoe. Her ears had pink rims but were white inside, with clean holes going into her head. She must wash more than other people, with a mother like Bette.

"I've never seen anyone so fat," he said.

"You don't have to," Verna said. "Walk with me, I mean."

"I will for a while." He looked ahead anxiously. "What was your name before? Before she married him?"

"Barrowclough. It's still my name. I'm not Muskie."

"You've got to be. What's it like? Living with him?"

Verna had a handkerchief threaded through a bangle on her wrist. She plucked it out and pushed it down the front of her dress. "My mum's scared of him," she said.

"Why'd she marry him, then?"

"She wasn't scared before, but she is now."

"What's he do?"

"He puts his hands like he's going to squeeze her all the time, and then he stops."

"Yeah?"

"He holds her face and turns it like it's something that comes off."

"Yeah?"

"And then he kisses her. He kisses me. Only on the cheek." She looked at him sharply. "I have to go away and wash my face."

"His scar," Colin said.

"It's like a maggot," Verna said. "He washes himself all the time. He makes Mum wash him in the bath."

"Yeah?"

"Don't you tell anyone," she said.

"I won't." He wanted her to stop and wanted her to go on. "Are you going to live in Mrs. Muskie's house when it's fixed?"

"We have to. He said."

"With Mrs. Muskie?"

"She smells."

"She's got a lot of money."

"So's he. That's why Mum got married to him. She told me she could make him do whatever she wants."

"But she can't?"

"No, she can't."

They walked a little further. Colin said, "You couldn't have worn your hat, anyway."

"I know." She made a move as if to touch her hair, then dropped her hand to her side. The bangle slid on her bony wrist. "What will they do to me?"

"I don't know. Nothing much." He did not believe it. The tough girls, the gang from over the creek, Betty Simpson, Nancy Rice, Jean Macnamee, would have all sorts of fun with Verna Muskie. And the boys would not leave Colin alone, either, unless he got away from her soon. He saw the roof of the school above the chestnut tree. Kids were going in the gate.

"You go in the front door, and the staff room is down the corridor."

Verna said nothing.

"Mr. Garvey will be there, not in his office. I've got to go now. I'm a bit late."

He ran ahead, half sideways, looking back at her as she advanced doggedly on the potholed footpath. "You'll be okay. You know the way," and he turned his back, ran well ahead, his bag flapping on his shoulders, through little kids who had stopped to watch Verna coming up the hill. He went through the gate and crossed the playground—paused at the door to watch her arrive, and heard the sudden quietness as everyone saw her. He went into his room and put his bag in his desk. The sums for the Monday test were chalked on the board, with the world map pulled down to cover most of them. Itchy's strap was hanging on its nail. Verna's shoes crossed the boards of the entrance hall and then were quiet. He looked out. She was standing by the coatrack, not knowing where to go. No one was looking in the door.

He went out quickly. "Here, down here," and led her down the corridor past the standard three and four room and Mr. Garvey's office to the staff room. He knocked. The door opened at once, and Miss Burgess looked out.

"What?" she said. "It better be important."

"Please, Miss Burgess, this is Verna Muskie. She's new."

He looked at Verna, who had her case open on her knee to find the letter. He went away, ran outside, found his friends. He had done it. He had got her into school without anyone seeing him. He joined the game of French cricket on the lower playground and did not see Verna again until the class filed into the standard six room after assembly. And there she was sitting in a front desk on the girls' side, with her fingers folded, looking straight ahead. No one said anything because Itchy Edgar was there, at his table, putting a new name in the roll. They stood quiet beside their desks waiting for him, and Verna, seeing this, got to her feet.

"Good," Itchy Edgar said. He looked up. "Sit."

Everyone sat. He called the roll, starting with the girls, and when he came to M he said, "The new girl is Verna Muskie. And I don't want any jokes about her hair. Do you hear that, Nancy Rice?"

"Yes, sir."

"Do you hear that, Austin Rice?"

"Yes, sir."

"She's been sick, that's why it's short. We'll see if it's affected her brains when we do the test," and he went on with the roll.

Colin always tried to finish halfway in the test so he would not have to change his seat by the window. So he got two sums wrong and four of the mental and four spelling words. They changed papers for marking, and Itchy checked them while they wrote their morning paragraph. Then Itchy read the placings out and people cleared their desks and shifted around. Girls first. Verna Muskie had made no mistakes. She stayed where she was in the front desk. Colin could not believe she had been so dumb. Nancy Rice and Betty Simpson, who had come last again, would get her for that. He looked at them sitting at the back, with their faces thick and eyes bright. The way they watched her made him feel sick. He did not care for Verna's face, either. It was white and pointed and still. She looked straight ahead, as though the blackboard and its sums were a corridor she might vanish along. Her cap of hair showed the thinness of her skull, which had the shape of a glass bowl. A tap with a spoon would splinter it. Colin turned away. He tried to make it easier by telling himself she was the fat man's daughter.

At interval Itchy Edgar kept her inside. But when lunchtime came, she had to go out. She sat by herself and, with Mr. Garvey on duty while they ate, no one went close to her. Colin got up to put his lunch paper in the rubbish tin. He made a curve on the way back, close to the girls' side, and risked saying to her, "Why did you have to get top in the test?" She looked at him, eyes blank, and shrugged. It must be like waiting for the firing squad. Then the bell rang, and Mr. Garvey went inside and people were free to move about.

Nancy Rice stood up. She stretched like a cat. Betty Simpson twirled around until her bloomers showed. And Jean Macnamee, with her flea-bitten legs, ran to join them. The boys, the Settlement gang, grinned and watched. "You're going to get it now, Mustpee," Austin Rice said.

At first they pretended to be friendly. "What did it feel like getting your head shaved?" Nancy said. But that sort of questioning soon stopped. Betty Simpson said, "I don't think you're a girl, you must be a boy."

"Girls don't have short hair," Jean said.

"Take her bloomers down and see," Austin Rice called out.

Jean Macnamee shrieked with glee and grabbed Verna's dress; but none of them had the nerve for it, with boys around. Instead they spun Verna, making her dizzy, faster, faster. Then they pushed her lazily back and forth until she had her balance back.

"We're going to give her green hair. Green hair," Nancy cried. She ran away around the side of the school, into the hollow where the drains came out. Betty and Jean held Verna by the arms, pulling her, pushing her, making her head wobble. Nancy came back. She carried two handfuls of green slime, holding it out to one side. It trailed gray water as she ran.

"Green hair," Jean Macnamee squealed. They held Verna still. A way opened for Nancy Rice and she ran through and stopped in front of Verna, who drew back her head at the dripping mess in Nancy's hands. "Don't," she said.

"You can get it permed," Betty Simpson said.

"We don't like kids with no hair," Nancy Rice said. "And dresses and pink bows and shoes and stuff. Or show-offs who come top of the class. Hold her still, Betty."

They had forgotten Verna's feet. She kicked suddenly. Her hard shoes cracked on Nancy's shins. Nancy cried out and dropped half the slime. But she pushed her head back in range, almost in Verna's face. "Now we'll make you eat it, Mustpee."

Verna spat in her face.

Then Miss Burgess's voice cried, "What's going on here?" She broke into the circle. Nancy had dropped the rest of the slime to wipe her face. Betty and Jean let Verna go.

"Verna Muskie spat in Nancy's face," Betty Simpson said.

"She just spat at her. For nothing, Miss Burgess," Jean said.

"She's a loony."

"She's got no hair."

"Quiet," Miss Burgess cried. "Now, Nancy. Where are you?"

"Here, Miss Burgess."

"Did she spit at you? What for?"

"I don't know, Miss Burgess. She just did it. I was only standing here."

"Not bullying her?"

"No, Miss Burgess."

"You. New girl. Did you spit at her?"

Verna stood alone. Her face was sharp and sour, and her teeth showed.

"Answer me. We won't have any spitting in this school."

"Yes."

"In her face?"

"Yes."

"All right. We'll teach you a lesson. Go and wait outside Mr. Garvey's office. And the rest of you clear off and play or I'll send Mr. Edgar out."

They broke up reluctantly. Colin kept away from Austin Rice's gang. He saw Verna walk into the school and Miss Burgess follow; watched Nancy and her friends chatter gleefully. He sat down on a seat and put his hands on his knees. He knew that now he had to do something. It was like having to swim across a deep pool in the creek without knowing what was on the bottom. No one else was going to help Verna. He had never seen anything like the sharpness on her face when she spat at Nancy. Suddenly she had seemed made of broken glass. Now he could not turn away from her, even though the Rice gang would get him.

After a moment he went into the school. He passed the standard four room and stood at Mr. Garvey's door. He heard Mr. Garvey's voice inside, asking questions. He heard him say, "I don't like strapping girls, but I will if I have to."

Colin knocked. The door sprang open.

"Yes, boy?"

"Please, sir," he said, and his dry mouth could make

no more sounds. Garvey towered over him, smelling of his pipe. Verna watched, expressionless.

"Please, sir . . ."

"You know the rule, Potter. You only come here for important things."

"Yes, sir. This is important, sir. Nancy Rice was putting slime on her for her hair."

"Slime?"

"From the drain. That's why she spat, sir. Betty Simpson and Jean Macnamee were holding her."

Garvey turned to Verna. "Is this true, girl?"

Verna answered woodenly, "Yes, sir."

"Slime from the drain?"

"Green slime. For green hair," Colin said.

"Girl?"

"Yes."

"All right, we'll see about this. Potter, send those three girls in to me."

"Me, sir?"

"Go on, boy. Do what you're told."

Teachers didn't understand a thing. He went into the playground and found them. "Mr. Garvey wants you," he said.

"You told, Pottsie."

"You snitched."

"You're a snitch."

They were like dogs snarling at him.

"You better go. He's waiting."

"I'm telling my brother," Nancy said.

He went away and lay down on a seat. His stomach felt

the way it had at Bellevue House, sitting down for dinner with the fat man. Somehow all of this was the fat man's fault.

By the end of lunchtime, the news was around the school. Nancy and Betty and Jean had got two cuts. Verna Muskie had got one for spitting. And Colin Potter had snitched. All afternoon he sat in class knowing that the Rice gang would get him. Usually they left him alone because he was good at football and cricket; because his father had been a boxer, too. But snitching changed all that.

They would get Verna as well. Across the room, she knew it. She looked at her red palm and sat still, waiting for the thing that must happen to her.

The bell rang. They went out into the playground. The slime lay where Nancy had dropped it, pasted on the asphalt, drying in the sun.

"Say your prayers, Pottsie," Austin Rice said. He went out the gate and down toward the bridge. It didn't matter if Colin tried to go the other way. They had scouts up there, too. Verna came out, carrying her case, which Colin looked at with pity.

"I'll walk with you," he said.

"You don't have to."

"They'll be waiting for both of us."

"They can do what they like."

He saw them lounging on the bridge. The girls were there, too. Somehow they were worse than the boys. All the boys would do was punch. Then he heard a horn hooting, and the Rice gang scattered. The Buick came through, riding high, with the fat man at the wheel. He took no notice of them but drove up the hill and pulled up at the school gates. He put his elbow on the window frame of the car and pushed his hat onto the back of his head.

"That gang down there wouldn't be waiting for you, would they, kid?"

Colin made no answer. He did not want to be saved by the fat man.

"Want me to go and deal with them?"

"No," Colin said.

"What about you, Vern? They causing you any trouble?"

"No," she said.

"Pity," said the fat man. "I could do with some exercise. Okay, hop in."

"Not me," Colin said.

"Yeah, you. It's your old man's orders. You're coming to do some work at the house."

"No."

"I can pick you up by the seat of your pants and chuck you in if you like." The worm in his cheek seemed to smile. "Vern, you sit beside me. Come on, your mother's there."

Verna got in the car. "You next, kid. You're not trying to make me mad, are you?"

Colin got in. They turned and went back down the hill, past the Rice gang standing sullenly at the side of the road. The fat man blew his horn.

"Lousy kids. I'd just as soon run over them," he said.

CHAPTER 6

Arm Wrestling

Colin had ridden in buses, but this was the first time he had been in a car. They went along Station Road, faster than a train, and onto the gravel road by the jam factory. Dust billowed behind them like smoke from a scrub fire. He would have enjoyed it except for the fat man spinning the wheel with his plump hands and ramming the gearstick up and down. Verna sat in the middle with her brown case on her lap. The fat man whistled one of Bette's tunes. He honked his horn musically at a dog. "Missed him," he said. "How'd school go, Vern?"

"All right."

"Get the strap?"

"Yes."

"You did? What for?"

"Spitting."

"You spat? I thought you were a lady, Vern."

"They tried to put slime on my head."

"Yeah?"

"From the drain."

"And what was the kid doing while that was going on? You help with the slime, kid?"

"No," Colin said.

"He told the headmaster. Or else I would have got the cuts even worse."

"You ratted, eh? Good on you. I'll let you have that shilling. Remind me."

They drummed over the bridge and turned into Millbrook Road. Mrs. Muskie's house slid out from behind its trees. Colin saw his father's bike leaning on the broken picket fence. The car stopped and he got out.

"'Round the back, kid. You'll find him there," the fat man said.

Colin went up the path. The front door had star-shaped fractures in its glass. The fat man went in, pushing Verna. Colin walked around the side path, past the col-ored window with its cabbagy rose, and heard his father whistling as he worked—the same tune the fat man had whistled in the car. Colin wanted to tell him to stop. He found him slashing blackberry by the collapsing shed.

"Gidday, son. Grab that rake and pull some of this stuff out of the way."

The slasher and the rake were brand new. The fat man was doing things properly. Colin put his bag by the tree and worked with his father. He wondered if his mother knew where he was. He did not like the way things were settling down—the way the fat man was becoming part of everything and nobody thought he was unusual.

"Dad?"

"Yeah?"

"How long will this take?"

"Well"—Laurie wiped sweat from his face—"I gotta get this stuff grubbed out and burned. Then I gotta knock down the shed. And shift all the rubbish by the creek."

"Shift the dump?"

"Yeah." Laurie was uneasy. "It won't take long."

"You're a carpenter, Dad."

"Then I can start on the house. Do my proper job. You can't turn down wages, Colin. It's better than relief."

"Is Grandpa going to do the drains?"

"When I get the section cleared. Ah, just what I need."

Verna had come out of the house with two glasses of lemonade. She waited while they drank. Laurie said, "Your hair's growing, Verna. You'll soon have your curls back, I reckon."

Verna smiled at him. It was the first time Colin had seen her smile. It took the sharpness out of her face and made it curvy and somehow sweet—too sweet for him. He had liked her better spitting at Nancy Rice.

"Sour lemonade," he said.

"I didn't make it."

"Who did?"

"His mother. She just squeezes lemons in and puts a bit of sugar."

"Not enough. Where'd she get the lemons?"

"He brought them."

"Where's he now?"

"Gone away. How do I know?" Her face was sharp again. He liked her better.

Bette came out of the house, bringing a wave of scented soap. "Verna said she liked school, Colin. Thank you for walking with her."

"That's all right."

"She says the other girls are nice."

"I didn't say nice," Verna said. "I said all right."

"I'm glad you're getting on, dear." She smiled at Laurie Potter. "Muscles," she said.

Laurie went red. "I better put my shirt on."

"I've been admiring you out the window. Men work so hard."

"I like to earn my money," Laurie said. He buttoned his shirt.

"Whistle while you work. Tra-la-la-la-la-la-la," Bette sang.

Verna blushed. "Come on, Mum." She took the empty glasses and went back to the house. Bette stayed a moment, admiring Laurie, then followed her.

"We should finish this job as quick as we can, Dad," Colin said.

"Yeah, let's," Laurie said.

They worked at the blackberry, Colin stepping carefully in his bare feet. He had not heard the fat man drive away but after a while heard him come back. Later he saw him in the house, at an upstairs window, watching them with his hands on the sill. He wore a little smile on his face, but it seemed something that might rub off and Colin could tell that he wasn't satisfied. He turned to talk to someone in the room—was it Mrs. Muskie number one or number two? Number one had looked out several times and cried, "Mind my hydrangeas." There were no hydrangeas, only dead bushes overgrown with blackberry.

"Dad," Colin whispered, nodding at the window, but

by the time Laurie looked, the fat man had gone. A moment later he opened the back door and came out carrying a kitchen chair. He put it on the path and sat down.

"Got to get out of there. Too many women." The late afternoon sun made his thin hair shine and his strips of scalp glisten like bone.

"The old lady's the worst," he said. "Always hunting."

"What for?" Laurie said.

"She reckons she's got some sovereigns in there, but she can't remember where she hid them. So she goes around looking under beds. Up the chimney. She even made me shift the wardrobe out."

"Nothing there?"

"Are you kidding? Golden sovereigns?" His eyes turned on Colin, quick as glass marbles in a ring. "You ever see a sovereign, kid?"

"No." Colin got the word out in a whisper. He saw Verna come out of the house and sit on the step. He said, "No," again, making it louder.

"Nor have I," the fat man said. "I reckon the old biddy's going bats."

Laurie frowned. He did not like this sort of talk in front of children. "We'll have to let this blackberry dry before we burn it," he said.

"Sure. No hurry." The fat man lit a cigarette. "She's got all sorts of beads in there, in a chamber pot. I never seen so much junk in me life. You want some beads, Vern?"

"No," Verna said.

"Don't blame you. They're only glass. I don't suppose Maisie would like some, Laurie?"

"No thanks," Laurie said. "She doesn't wear beads."

"There's rings and stuff. Bangles. Brooches."

"No."

"Only asking. I'll tell you what, Laurie, that place in there is a bloody shambles. Sorry, blooming. You never seen so much dust in your life. Spiderwebs. Mason bees. You don't reckon Maisie would come and lend a hand? I'd pay her for it."

"No chance."

"Bette's so blooming useless. Says she didn't marry me to be a kitchen maid."

"Maisie's not a kitchen maid, either."

"Hey, no offense. It was just an idea. How'd you like to be a kitchen maid, Vern? Give you sixpence."

Verna stood up and went into the house.

"Too many women," the fat man repeated. "And all of them useless." He put his palms up quickly at Laurie. "Leaving Maisie out of it, of course." He smoked his cigarette down to the butt, then stubbed it out on the path and picked up his chair. "Too much sun out here." He turned to the door but stopped and felt in his pocket. "By the way, kid, here's your bob." He flicked a shilling at Colin.

Colin saw it coming, but could not move his hand fast enough. The coin vanished into the blackberry vines.

"Now you'll have to hunt for it," the fat man said. He went inside.

"I don't want it, Dad," Colin said.

"Leave it. We'll find it soon enough."

Laurie worked on, and when he uncovered the shilling handed it to Colin without a word. Colin put it in his pocket. Soon after that they went home, Laurie doubling Colin on the bike. The Buick passed them, turning onto the bridge, with Bette and Verna sitting in front with the fat man. Herbert Muskie played a tune on his horn. Bette waved, but Verna ignored them.

"How'd she get on at school?" Laurie asked.

"They tried to put slime on her hair."

"Who, the girls?"

"Nancy Rice. I went and told Mr. Garvey."

"Austin Rice will get you for that, I suppose."

"Yes."

"Straight left, Colin. Right cross."

"Yes."

Maisie was laying the table when they came in. They kissed her and washed their hands and sat down to eat. Maisie asked about Verna, too. Colin told her that she was all right; she had come top in the test. He said he would walk with her tomorrow.

"I wish she wouldn't wear those stupid shoes, though," he said.

"You'll have shoes one day, my boy."

"But I won't wear them to school."

"Yes you will."

Colin did not answer. He took the shilling from his pocket and pushed it across the table. "Here, Mum. You can have that."

"Where did you get it?"

"From him. For walking with her."

Maisie turned to Laurie. "I don't want Herbert Muskie giving us things all the time."

"Nor do I. Just my wages."

"He came around here this afternoon."

"Here? When?"

"About four o'clock. I didn't want to let him in, but he brought me these." She got up and fetched a paper bag from the scullery. She put it on the table and gave the corner a jerk. Half a dozen oranges tumbled out.

"I didn't want to take them," Maisie said.

"Why'd he bring them?"

"I don't know. He said he thought I'd like them." She gathered the oranges, but left one on the table beside the salt.

"He's got a cheek coming here when I'm not home," Laurie said.

"I told him that. He didn't stay, Laurie. I told him to go."

"But you kept the oranges."

"He wouldn't take them. Besides . . ."

"Yeah?"

"Colin should have fruit."

"I don't want them," Colin said.

"We haven't had oranges for years."

How had the fat man known that she loved oranges—that oranges were what she missed more than anything? It was as if he knew every secret, as if he had some power over them. The orange glowed on the table. It was warm and full of juice—and how could it fit with Herbert

Muskie, with hair pasted on his head and the worm in his cheek? Colin could not work it out. But his mother peeled the orange after tea and broke it into segments, and he ate his share. He had not remembered that oranges were so sweet.

He took one to school the next day. When it was peeled, he gave half to Verna Muskie.

The Rice gang got him, of course. But it wasn't too bad. Just a few punches, and a hammerlock that hurt, and Austin Rice slapping his face back and forth, while Banks and Miller held him by the arms. There was no chance of straight left, right cross. His father had forgotten how things were. Colin's ears rang for an hour afterward. His mouth was swollen, but his mother hardly noticed. She was too much concerned about the tear in his shirt.

Verna Muskie had a worse time. The girls kept at her for the rest of the week, with bumps and trips, nothing the teachers could see. One day, when the class was playing rounders on the top field, someone stole her red shoes. She found them in the can in the girls' room and there was no way to get them out. The next day she wore sandals, which was a little better.

Sometimes the fat man met them after school and drove them to Mrs. Muskie's, where Verna was helping her mother clean the house. Verna did most of the work. Her mother did not want to spoil her hands. She might, she said, have to play piano for a living again, who knows? She only said that when the fat man wasn't there.

Mrs. Muskie prowled about, talking to herself. She

hunted for her lost sovereigns and watched Laurie from behind the curtains. "You've buried them," she cried one day; sometimes she came outside and dug for them with a garden trowel.

Herbert Muskie was away for much of the time. He drove to Auckland, down the Great North Road. "Business," he said, when he came back. He brought bags of chocolates for his mother and calmed her down. He walked her up the stairs with his arm wrapped around her, through the colored light from the stained-glass window, and put her into bed and pulled her blankets up and had Bette bring her a cup of tea.

"He doesn't love her, he's only pretending," Verna said.

"Why?"

"To get her money. He leaves the rat poison out on purpose, I'll bet. He wants her to take it one day."

Laurie had grubbed the blackberries out and demolished the shed. He had cleared away the rubbish from the creek bank, and the fat man had borrowed the sawmill truck to cart it away. The rats had lost their home and tried to come into the house, so he laid poison for them—and Colin believed it, he was hoping his mother would eat some instead of chocolate one day.

"He leaves it on the bench," Verna said. "She took some out and sniffed it yesterday, and he only laughed. He said she'd have a bellyache if she swallowed that. He told her not to mix it in her tea."

They were sheltering from rain down by the creek, where the rubbish had been cleared away. Laurie and

Grandpa, who was digging out the drains, had run for cover into the house.

"There's no rats left. He's got them all," she said.

"There's one there," Colin said, pointing.

"No, there's not." She looked at him with scorn. "Rats don't scare me."

He was disappointed that his joke hadn't worked. Verna had begun to fascinate him. He liked the way she was tough and pretty at the same time. He looked out from the cover of their tree at rain pocking the surface of the creek. "When your hair grows long . . ."

"Yes?" She looked at him sharply.

"Maybe you can be my girlfriend, eh?"

"Who wants to be your girlfriend? I like my hair the way it is, anyway."

"I bet you don't. We can go to the pictures. On Saturdays."

"Does Rice Pudding and her friends go there?"

"Sometimes."

"Well, I'm not going."

"No, I guess . . ."

"You've got to like my hair the way it is."

"Sure. I do."

"Say it, then."

"I like your hair."

"All right. So I'll be your girlfriend. But only here. Nowhere else."

"You mean, by the creek."

"What do you think he'd do if he found out?"

"Yeah."

"I don't want him knowing anything about me."

"Nor do I." Colin shivered. Then he said, "Do we kiss or something?"

"No, we don't. I hate kissing. He kisses her."

"Your mother?"

"He makes her sit on his knee and kiss him in his ears."

"Ears?"

"He gets lipstick in them, and she has to clean it out with her handkerchief."

"Have you seen him shaving?"

"No."

"Have you seen his razor?"

"No. Why? This tree's no good. I'm getting wet."

He wanted to tell her about his first meeting with the fat man and about the theft of Mrs. Muskie's sovereigns, but that might make it worse for her, living with him. While he was trying to decide, she ran from the tree for a thicker one along the bank, but halfway there she slipped where Laurie had dragged the rubbish up. It had become a mud slide and Verna went down sideways, then head-first, into the creek. She vanished under the green surface but popped up like a cork, with her hair flattened on her skull. She clawed at the bank.

Colin scrambled down the bank, grabbing hold of roots. He worked his way along to her. She had dug her fingers into the mud and was holding on. He grabbed a root with one hand and reached out with the other.

"Grab hold."

She made a lunge at him and he hauled her clear of

the mud slide until she was able to climb into the tree roots. He helped her to the top of the bank.

"Why didn't you swim?"

"I can't." She was shivering. Her face had turned as white as paper.

"You better go inside and dry yourself."

They ran for the house, jumping across the new-dug drains. She opened the door and ran in, and Colin, behind her, heard Bette shriek. He did not want to go where the fat man was, but the rain fell thicker, so he stepped in and half closed the door.

"Drowned rats," the fat man said. He laughed.

"You all right, Colin?" Laurie said.

"She fell in the creek."

"What she'll get is a hiding for that," the fat man said.

"No," Bette said. She had wrapped Verna in her arms. "I told her not to go near the creek."

"Take it easy, Herbie," Laurie said.

The fat man turned his eyes on him. "Who said it's any of your business?"

The men were at the table, drinking beer. Mrs. Muskie walked about, moaning distractedly. She opened cupboards and rattled tins and crockery inside.

"Shut up, Ma. Put a sock in it." The fat man was edgy and sour. He was dangerous. "Take her upstairs," he said to Bette. "Take them both."

But Bette took only Verna. The fat man stood up. He seized his mother by the arms and sat her in a chair. "Sit and keep quiet. Kid, you're treading dirt in. Wipe your feet."

Colin went outside, although the rain came down just

as hard, and washed his feet under the garden tap. He would have gone around to the front and sheltered on the porch, but he wanted to be with his father—he felt that he, and Grandpa, too, were somehow under threat. When he went back they were talking about boxing. He went around the table to stand by Laurie, passing Mrs. Muskie on the way. He caught the sour smell of her, and heard her rhythmical groaning like the purring of a cat except that it sounded of distress. It kept time with her rocking in her chair.

"A good wrestler will always beat a boxer," the fat man said. "All he's got to do is get a grip."

"No," Laurie said, "because a boxer hits him coming in. A wrestler's wide open for a punch."

"Sure, he'll take a few. You always take a few to get in close. But once you get your hands on, it's all over. A wrestler will break a boxer up, with his pansy gloves. He'll tear off his arms, eh, and feed 'em to the cat. What you say, Ma?"

"Those men are digging in my garden."

"They're digging drains, not for sovereigns, Ma." He winked at Colin—"Sovereigns"—and spiraled his finger at his temple. Then he grinned at Laurie. "Tell you what, why don't you and me try it out? I'll be the wrestler, eh, and you can be the boxer. There's room here."

"No, Dad," Colin said.

"I don't fight anymore."

"You can be bare knuckles. Even it up. We'll push the table back against the wall, make a ring. Get up, Ma."

"Someone will only get hurt, Herbie," Laurie said.

"I'm used to getting hurt. I can stand a bit of pain to prove I'm right."

"No fighting," Grandpa said. "It only makes bad blood. Tell you what, why don't you have an arm wrestle, eh? Boxer against wrestler, eh, eh?"

"I don't mind that," Laurie said.

"Arm wrestling? Well, sure, why not? I seen a bit of that in me time," the fat man said. A cruel little smile played on his mouth, and the worm made a sideways jump. "Just to make it interesting, how about we each put in ten bob? Winner takes all."

"Ten bob?"

"Ha!" Grandpa said. "Take it, Laurie. If Herbie wants to chuck his money away."

Mrs. Muskie stood up and searched in the cupboards again. No one took any notice of her. They cleared an end of the table and placed two chairs. The fat man took his jacket off. Yellow braces held his trousers up. His torso was rounded like a melon. Laurie was a beanpole beside him. His hands were bigger, though, and his arms more muscular. Colin put his hope in that. When they clasped hands, the brown one almost swallowed up the white.

"You can be referee, eh, Pops," the fat man said.

"Sure thing," Grandpa said. "When I say go . . . both ready? Go."

Colin knew at once that his father would lose. His forearm was longer, and he had to bend his wrist. The fat man's arm was immovable. His face colored to a yellow-pink from which the scar stood out in a ridge, white as dough, but he showed no other sign of strain. Laurie was fitter, and stronger in his arm, but the fat man was able to get eighteen stone behind his push. Slowly he levered Laurie over. Then he let him come up and gain an inch or two. Colin saw that he was playing. Laurie knew it, too. Sweat had broken out on his face.

"Laurie, you're not bad for a country boy," the fat man said.

"Gone, gone," Mrs. Muskie moaned, rattling plates.

"But I been in a hard school. Want to give in?"

"No," Laurie gritted. Perhaps he thought his fitness might count in the end.

"I seen arms get broken in this game," the fat man said. He stayed rock still, then reached his left hand into his pocket and dabbed his cheeks with his handkerchief. "But if I break yours, you won't be able to finish my weatherboards, eh?"

"No giving cheek to your opponent," Grandpa cried.

"Shut up, Pops," the fat man said. He held Laurie still for a moment longer, then forced his hand down easily and laid it on the table. "Ten bob to me."

Laurie looked stricken. He could not look at Colin or Grandpa. He seemed to shrink as if some of his weight was lost.

"I'll take it out of your wages," the fat man said.

"Yes. All right."

"It's a long time from Loomis school, eh, Laurie?"

"Laurie would still beat you in a fight," Grandpa said.

But Colin knew he was wrong. The fat man would do what he had said: get in close and squeeze and twist, break Laurie up. It was as if he had started already.

"You reckon? You want to try, Laurie?"

"No. No fights," Laurie said.

"I'll go easy on you."

Laurie shook his head. He took his glass of beer and drank a sip. He did not seem able to gulp anymore.

"Ma, sit down," the fat man said. "There's no sovereigns." He grinned at Laurie. "You want to have a turn against my ma? Get your ten bob back? I'll tell her to go easy, too."

"Hey," Grandpa said, "there's no call for cheek. We're all friends here."

Laurie worked his arm, getting its strength back. "What's biting you, Herbie?" And perhaps there would have been a fight, but a knocking on the front door brought the fat man's head swinging around.

"What the hell . . . ?"

He screeched back his chair and left the kitchen with Mrs. Muskie after him, still talking to herself. Looking on an angle across the hall, Colin saw him swing the front door open. Two women with dripping umbrellas stood on the porch. Clyde Muskie peered from behind them.

"Herbie," he said, grinning uncertainly, "here's Olive and Dora. We thought we'd come and visit you and Mum."

"Well, if it ain't me sisters," the fat man said. "Ain't that great?"

The sisters were tall women with none of Clyde's uncertainty. The one in front sprang her umbrella half open and shook it again, spraying the fat man with water. Her hair bushed out from under her hat.

"Herbert, what makes you think you can come back and live in this house? Without so much as by your leave?"

Colin could only see the fat man's back, but he felt him smile, felt the worm wriggle in his cheek.

"Come in or stay out, Olive. Make up your mind. I'm closing the door."

"We're coming in. We've got more right than you. Who are these people?"

The fat man closed the door. He looked at Colin and Laurie and Grandpa peering from the kitchen and winked at them. "Me carpenter. Me drainlayer. Remember the Potters, Olive? They're working for me. And that lady up there on the stairs is me wife. And that's me daughter. Bette and Verna. Say hallo."

"Wife? You've got no wife. Who'd marry you? She's your fancy lady. How dare you bring her into Mother's house?"

"Married her in the registry office, Olive. I'd have asked you both if I'd thought you'd come. Want to see the certificate? Fetch it, Bette. But hey, I haven't finished my introductions. This lady standing here is my Mum. Remember her? It's a long time since you met, eh, Olive?"

The other sister pushed her head out on her long neck. "We don't come because we're not welcome," she hissed. "But that doesn't excuse you. We know what you're after."

"What am I after, Dora? Her sovereigns? Tell them, Ma."

"They stole them. You stole them," Mrs. Muskie

cried. "These women came and stole my sovereigns. Where have you put them?"

"Mother, we stole nothing," Olive said. "But Herbert has come to steal your house. And Dora and I are not going to let him."

The fat man laughed. It had an ugly sound—the gravel in the chute sound Colin knew. He stood close to his father. He looked at Verna at the top of the stairs, close to her mother. No one was safe from the fat man. But at least it was Olive and Dora and Clyde he was after now.

"What I'm doing," he said, "I'm looking after Mum's business affairs. Not that there's much of them. But what about you, eh, Olive, eh, Dora? Waiting for her to die, am I right? Then you'll be out here like a pack of hungry dogs."

"How dare you?"

"I dare anything," the fat man said.

"We'll get the police. We'll get you thrown out of here."

"Too late, me lovely sisters." He turned to Bette on the stairs. "Aren't they lovely girls? Look at them. They don't come to see their ma for ten bloody years. But when they hear I'm home, they're out here in a flash to look after her. Real queens."

"Herbie, we got some rights," Clyde said.

"Who says? You got no rights. I'm the one with rights now, and I'll tell you what they are. I run things for Mum. Me. Herbert Muskie. We went to see a lawyer and all the business side is handed over to me. I'm the manager. Tell 'em, Ma."

"Yes," Mrs. Muskie cried, "Herbert has come home. I always knew he'd come. But where have my sovereigns gone?"

"Mother," Olive said, stepping toward her. The old lady lifted her hands to ward her off.

"Stay away. I've made a will. It's all for Herbert now. He's the only one who cares. What have you done with my sovereigns?"

"Oh, Mother."

"Oh, Mother," the fat man parroted.

"We love you, Mother," Dora said. "We've come to save you."

"From me," the fat man said, and laughed, keeping in check an ugly rage. "Well, now I'll do some saving of my own. Out, out." He moved at them and drove them back, Olive and Dora and Clyde; threw the front door open. "Out you go." Then he saw the sawmill truck parked at the gate. "What, Clyde, you drove them around here in the truck? Me stuck-up sisters? I'll bet they loved that, eh?"

"Herbie . . ."

But the fat man seized him and held him helpless. He rummaged in his pockets and came out with a key. "Well, they can walk back, rain or not. Because I'm taking the truck. I've got a buyer."

"You can't," Clyde said. "I can't run the mill without a truck."

"The mill's closing. It's closed. It's costing money. The mill doesn't open tomorrow."

"You can't do that."

"I can. I just did. Why should Ma and me keep the mill just so you can have a free ride? Out you go. Out, Olive."

"But listen—"

"Out, Dora."

He slammed the door and turned them into shadows behind the fractured glass.

The fat man laughed. "Showed 'em, eh? Got rid of them." He stretched his yellow braces and let them snap back against his belly. "Come 'ere, Bette, and give me a kiss." But Bette seized Verna and fled with her under the stained-glass window into a bedroom.

Colin and Laurie and Grandpa went back into the kitchen.

"Can we go home, Dad?"

"It's still raining."

"I don't care."

"Yeah, let's go."

Laurie packed his tool kit. They heard the fat man walk up the stairs and heard a door open and heard him laugh. In a moment Verna came down. She sat at the table and looked at no one. Mrs. Muskie came in and took up her search.

"We're going, Verna," Colin said.

She made no reply.

"I'll see you tomorrow." She was still in her damp dress. All her other clothes were at Bellevue House.

"Will she be all right, Dad?" he said as they went out the gate.

"Yeah, I think so. The old lady's there. Her mother's there."

That counted for nothing. But there was not a thing Colin could do. Olive and Dora and Clyde walked ahead of them, huddled under two umbrellas. The rain stopped as they turned onto the bridge. Grandpa caught up with them and walked with Clyde. Colin and his father went the other way.

"Can he really close the mill, Dad?"

"I suppose."

"Why?"

"He doesn't need a reason. But it's true what he says, it's not making any money. All it does is keep Clyde in a job."

"What will Clyde—Mr. Muskie—do?"

"I don't know."

"Do you really think there's a will? And Herbert Muskie gets everything?"

"If there's anything to get."

Colin nearly told him about the sovereigns. Instead, he said, "Do you have to work for him, Dad?"

"It's wages, son."

His father was defeated. The fat man had beaten him, more than just with arm wrestling. He had made him smaller, somehow.

"Has he been seeing Mum again?"

"No, I warned him off."

Colin did not believe in a warning-off, not anymore.

"Did you really bully him at school?"

"Yeah, a bit."

"Is that why he wants to get us now?"

"He doesn't want to get us, Colin. I don't know . . ."

His father wouldn't talk about it anymore.

Colin took his hand as they walked along, and Laurie, who would normally have thought it was sissy, held it and did not seem to mind.

CHAPTER 7

The Fat Man Gets Serious

The sawmill closed. The fat man sold the truck. Laurie worked at the house, stripping rotten weatherboards and putting new ones in. He replaced floorboards here and there, rehung the sticking doors, got the windows running smoothly in their frames. He climbed a long ladder to the roof, removed sheets of rusty iron, and hammered new ones in. Grandpa Potter finished the drains. But still the old lady lived alone in the house while Verna and Bette and Herbert Muskie boarded at Bellevue House.

By the time of the May school holidays, Laurie was almost ready to start the painting. He had burned the old paint off with a blowtorch, working on a scaffold high up the walls. Colin helped with sandpaper, working at ground level, and Verna gave a hand now and then. Colin liked working alongside her. Her hair had grown two inches and was starting to curl. But he didn't care about that anymore, he liked her how ever it was. "Lovebirds," Grandma said in her sour way. Bette Muskie wasn't pleased about them, either. She did not like her daughter running around with a barefoot boy.

As for the fat man, he did not seem to notice. He was

away most of the time. He drove off along the Great North Road each morning and often was not home till after dark. The truth, which came out later, was that he had become a receiver of stolen goods, working with the man who had bought Laurie's cups. Perhaps he did some burglary, too—no one knows. He always had plenty of money. But whatever he was up to, his other game, his deeper game, was being played in Loomis.

He and Grandpa Potter set up a little sly-grog shop, working out of a shed at the disused mill. The fat man brought crates of beer from Auckland in his car—you could get six dozen bottles in the boot and another four, hidden under a blanket, on the backseat. He carted the beer and took the profits while Grandpa, on wages, did the selling. They explained his presence at the mill by saying that he was nightwatchman there. All this came out later, too. And Grandpa was arrested and served a month in prison, which would have pleased the fat man, although it was Laurie and Maisie he was really after. But our story is getting ahead of itself. We must go back and say what happened to Mrs. Muskie.

"He locks her in her bedroom at night," Verna said. "He says it's so she won't burn down the house. You can hear her crying in there."

"Someone should tell Clyde."

"He makes Mum empty her chamber pot when we go around. At least he bought a new chamber pot."

"Why don't you and your mother run away?"

"Mum's too scared. She says he'll come and find us."

Sometimes the fat man forgot to lock the door—or

perhaps he left it unlocked on purpose. Then Mrs. Muskie searched the house for her sovereigns. She pinned on her hat, lit a kerosene lamp, and dug at Grandpa's new drains with her trowel. Someone must have told Olive and Dora. They made another visit and tried to smuggle Mrs. Muskie with them to the train, but the fat man came home and chased them away.

Autumn came. The weather was steamy and wet. Maisie Potter bought Colin some shoes and insisted that he wear them to school. So he set off with them on his feet but took them off around the first bend in the road. He carried them in his schoolbag all day and put them on just before he reached home again. Verna, too, was learning to run barefooted. The Rice gang had lost interest in her now that her hair had started to grow. Several times she and Colin went to the pictures on Saturday afternoon. They held hands in the dark. It was known in Loomis school that they were girlfriend and boyfriend and they got kidded about it for a while, but that stopped, too. Colin would have been happy in these days if it hadn't been for his father not alive in the way he had been, and for the fat man, always there even when he was away in Auckland.

In the holidays he helped all day, sanding the baseboards of the house. He and his father started work at eight in the morning and sometimes heard Mrs. Muskie calling to be let out of her room. Then Colin would slide a window up and climb inside. He ran up the stairs past the colored window, turned the key in her lock, and ran back again. She prowled the house. The fat man did not seem to mind when he arrived. "Don't get too smart, kid," was all he said.

They rode down on the bike one morning after a night of rain. The sky had cleared, the day would be muggy and hot. They both worked with their shirts off, although dust from the sanding soon caked Colin's skin. Mrs. Muskie made no sound in the house, which meant that the fat man had not locked her in. Colin wondered if he would come today, or if Bette and Verna would walk around. He liked Verna to see him working hard.

"Got to have a pee, Dad," he called.

"Have one for me," Laurie answered from high on the scaffold.

Colin grinned. His father sounded more the way he had been. He went down to the back of the section, past the bare patch where the shed had stood and the grubbed earth that would turn into a lawn one day—so the fat man said. Already it was growing weeds. He stood out of sight from the house and peed at the creek, hoping he wouldn't poison the eels. It wasn't till he was buttoning up that he noticed something—what was it, a bunch of dried flowers?—caught against the bank where the pool curved out of sight. He looked harder and saw that it floated on a small island, brown or green. Then it came properly into focus, and it was Mrs. Muskie's hat. The fat man must have thrown it away—he had threatened to.

Colin thought he might rescue it and give it to her. He moved several steps along the top of the bank. Then he saw something under the water—a dull gleam like the belly of an eel. It took a moment, like the hat, for it to come clear—to become a human leg, with a slipper on the foot. He almost screamed. He stumbled partway down the bank, beside the mud slide where the tip had been, for a better look. Mrs. Muskie came into view, with the top part of her body floating facedown and her arms hanging deep in the water as though she were reaching for her sovereigns down there. Her legs were deep down, too, in the green pool, lit with the dull gleam Colin had seen. Her thin hair floated like gray weed, with a single hat pin, caught in a knot, weighing an edge of it down.

Colin clawed his way up the bank. "Dad," he screamed. "Mrs. Muskie's in the creek. Dad, Dad."

Laurie came down the scaffold like a monkey. He ran to the creek, saw the body, climbed down. He grabbed a shoulder and tried to lift. Mrs. Muskie swung around heavily.

"Is she dead, Dad?"

"Yeah, she's dead. She's cold as ice. Go and get some help, Colin. We've got to get her out."

"Dad, I can hear his car. The fat man's coming."

The sound of slamming doors came from the road.

"Stop him. Don't let him see," Laurie said.

Colin ran back past the house. The fat man and Bette and Verna were halfway along the front path.

"Busy already, kid?" the fat man said.

"Don't go around there. Dad said not to go," Colin cried.

The fat man understood instantly. How had he been so quick? He gave a bellow—rage or grief?—and swept Colin aside, bowling him among the brittle hydrangeas on the lawn. He ran as lightly as a sprinter, knees high, belly thrust forward like a chest.

"Ma," he bellowed. His hat flew backward off his head.

Colin picked himself up and followed, with Verna at his heels and Bette Muskie twittering behind.

The fat man reached the top of the bank. He saw Laurie tugging at the body and gave a roar. "Get your hands off, Potter. I'll kill you if you touch her."

He plunged down the mud slide like a woolbale in a chute, into the water, under the water; reached his mother's body in two wallowing heaves. Laurie drew back. The fat man seized her and seemed to fight. He got her in a wrestling hold and pushed and lifted her onto the bank. He struck at Laurie when he tried to help. At last he had her out of the water, although it leaked from her, and from him, and ran in streams. He sat and held her in his arms, with her gray nightie draped in folds and her white feet sliding on the mud. (The slipper had come off. It sank slowly in the pool.) He hugged her against his chest and dripped on her and let out cries like the mooing of a cow.

Laurie climbed the bank.

"Colin, get on my bike and get the police. You better say to bring the doctor, too."

Colin rode along Millbrook Road, over the bridge, into Loomis, to the police station. He told Constable Dreaver what had happened, then rode back as fast as he could. The constable's bike caught him at the gate. They hurried in together and found Laurie and Bette and

Verna still at the top of the bank.

"He won't let anyone go near," Laurie said.

Herbert Muskie was quiet now. He sat with his mother in his arms and seemed to stare into the pool, where her hat was floating toward the far bank.

Constable Dreaver climbed down to him. "Mr. Muskie." He touched him on the shoulder. Herbert turned his face and snarled, so the constable came back.

"We'll wait for the doctor. Who found her?"

"Colin did."

"She was floating down there against the bank," Colin said.

"I'll need to see you later. You better go home now. And the lady and the girl. We'll have to get them up from there, Laurie."

"It's not going to be easy," Laurie said.

"She must have slipped down in the night."

"Yeah."

"I can get her hat if you like," Colin said.

"No, you go home," Laurie said. "Tell your mother I'll get back when I can."

"Colin, take Verna with you. I don't want her here. I'm going to wait in the house," Bette said.

They walked back together. "He's gone mad," Colin said.

"He was mad before. How bad does it hurt when you drown?"

"I don't know." He was worried about his father, so close to Herbert Muskie, and was relieved when he saw the doctor's car crossing the bridge.

They told Maisie what had happened. She made Colin wash and put a clean shirt on.

"I didn't touch her."

"Never mind. Verna, are you all right?"

"I've never seen a dead person before."

"Try not to dwell on it, dear. How's Herbert taking it?"

"He's holding her as though she's still alive."

They sat on the front steps and ate bread and jam.

"If he loves her, why did he lock her up?" Colin said.

"He's just pretending," Verna said.

"No, he's not. You couldn't cry and yell and do that stuff."

"What about the rat poison? I bet he pushed her down the bank."

"Why?"

"For her money. For the house. Because he hates her. I don't know. You should have looked for footprints."

Colin could not remember seeing any.

"Now it's too late. He didn't come in till after two o'clock last night. I heard the clock. Then I heard him coming up the stairs, and him and Mum . . ."

"What?"

"Nothing."

But he knew. And two o'clock, and coming up the stairs: He suddenly knew that she was right, the fat man had drowned his mother. But what about the tears rolling on his cheeks and the way he had hugged her on his chest, like a doll? That was real.

"I think he's going to get us all," he said.

Sitting there on the steps, in the autumn sun, he told Verna about his first meeting with Herbert Muskie and about stealing the sovereigns.

"You should have told someone. The police."

"I couldn't. He said I helped him. We'd be accomplices."

"He made you, so it's not your fault."

"Then he went away, so it was all right. I didn't know he was coming back."

"You've got to tell now."

"No. Because . . ." He knew the trouble he'd be in, and how upset his mother would be. No one would believe him, anyway. And then, when it was over, the fat man would come. . . .

"When Dad gets the painting done, we don't have to go back anymore. So it's all finished."

"What about Mum? What about me?"

"You should run away."

But Colin did not believe in that. The fat man would find them just like Verna said.

"I'm so frightened of him," she whispered.

He put his arm around her and did not take it away until he saw his father walking up the street with Bette, pushing his bike.

Maisie came out to the porch.

"They got her up. They took her away," Laurie said.

"How's Herbie?"

"No one can get near him," Bette said.

"He's sitting at the table in the kitchen."

"Drinking beer."

"He won't let the doctor look at him. Won't even talk to Bill Dreaver."

"I don't know what he'll do now. But something terrible," Bette said, wringing her hands.

"Come into the kitchen, Bette. Come on. I'll make us all some tea," Maisie said.

"I'll have to go back there, but I don't want to."

"Come on." She took her away.

Colin and Verna went around to the back of the house with Laurie, who put his bike in the shed.

"Do they know how it happened, Dad?" Colin said.

"Near enough. She slid down the bank."

"Where the tip was?"

"Yeah. She must have been looking for her sovereigns, damn things."

"In the rain?"

"If you're barmy, Colin . . . anyhow, I guess she slipped. We found her lamp sunk in the creek. And her trowel. Poor old dame, she tried to climb up. There's finger marks in the mud."

"Footprints?"

"No. Everyone's been walking around at the top of the bank. You can't say how she went down. But after a while she got too weak . . . try not to think about it, eh? Both of you."

In the afternoon Colin told Constable Dreaver how he had found Mrs. Muskie's body. He even said he'd gone there for a pee, but the constable said that didn't need to go in the report. He said that Colin had done very well, and Laurie, too.

Colin wanted to say, "Maybe someone pushed her," but he didn't dare. He wanted to say, "Ask Verna what time he came home."

Herbert Muskie drove back to Bellevue House and locked himself in his room and didn't come out until next day. Then he arranged the funeral beautifully, all Loomis said. He didn't cry at the service or the graveside. Clyde cried. Three of the four sisters came and they cried, too. But it was Herbert Muskie who got the house and the shops and the money—although no one knew if there was very much of that.

He shifted to his mother's house with Bette and Verna, so Grandpa and Grandma lost their boarders at Bellevue House. Laurie kept on with the painting. When it was finished, he painted the roof.

"Forget about the bathroom and the toilet, they can wait," the fat man said. "I want you to build a new shed. I gotta have a place to store some stuff."

"Sure, Herbie," Laurie said, relieved to have the work.

Colin and Verna met on the bridge and walked to school each morning. "He hits Mum," Verna said. "She's got black eyes all the time. That's why she doesn't go out."

"Does he hit you?"

"Not yet. He's bought that piano from your grandpa."

"Yes, I know."

"He made her play it all last night."

"And sing?"

"Ireland must be heaven, for my mother came from there."

"He's not Irish."

"It doesn't matter. He goes into her bedroom and sits on her bed."

"Does he cry?"

"He hugs her pillow. Sometimes he sleeps in there. He took that chamber pot of beads down to the creek and threw them in. Her false teeth, too."

"He still killed her, though."

"I know. I'm scared he's going to do something to Mum and me."

Colin wanted to save her, but could not think how. They could run away. They could hide in the hut. But he only had to think of the fat man, and his ideas blew away. Laurie Potter had almost started looking up to him. Herbert Muskie had money. Laurie seemed to go no further than that. Colin saw his family was caught in a trap: Grandpa, his father, his mother, too (the fat man dropped off bags of fruit and she didn't say no). And Verna was caught. He was caught. But catching would not be enough. Sometime soon the fat man would want to do something with the people in his trap.

"We're going 'round to Herbie's for a housewarming party," Laurie said.

"Who?"

"You and me and Colin. Saturday. And Mum and Dad."

"I don't want to go." Lately Maisie seemed more

frightened of the fat man than disapproving.

"Ah, come on, Maise. Just for a drink. Bette will be there. It's no wild party."

They walked around early in the afternoon. Colin wore his shoes. "They're lasting well," Maisie said. Bette opened the door and asked them in. They had not seen her for several weeks. Even Laurie, working on the new shed, did not see her. She went upstairs if he had to come into the kitchen.

"Bette," Maisie said, "what's happened to you?"

"I haven't been well. I've been sick."

"But your face?"

"I slipped over in the bath. I'm sorry, I thought the powder would cover it."

"Bette—"

"Don't say anything. Don't let Herbert know you can see."

"A blind man could see."

"Please, don't. He's coming. Oh, Herbert, they've arrived, isn't that nice?"

It was afternoon tea rather than a party. They sat in the living room, still with its bulging wallpaper and its ragged scrim, while Bette wheeled around a tea trolley loaded with cakes. Colin had never seen so many kinds. Bette had not baked them; the fat man had brought them from Auckland in his car. "You gotta know where to go," he said when Maisie exclaimed. "There's sandwiches, too, with ham and mustard. Have one, Laurie. You like sandwiches."

"I like 'em," Grandpa said. "Shoot 'em over here.

What we need with these, Herbie, is a beer."

"You're having tea. Beer is later on. This is a party in memory of my mum. Pour it, Bette, don't stand there."

Bette poured while Verna took her place at the tea trolley. Colin ate a chocolate meringue. He ate a piece of strawberry sponge. The fat man smiled at him.

"You're not going to get sick this time, are you, kid? Give him another piece, Verna."

Verna ate nothing. And nobody spoke much, not even Grandpa. Colin half-expected to see Mrs. Muskie in the room, see her opening cupboards in her hat. The fat man was conscious of her, too, for he said, "Mum would have liked this. All her old plates out and her trolley and cups. She always had a sweet tooth. She liked chocolate sponge. Play a tune for Mum, Bette. Come on out here."

They took their cups and plates of cake into the entrance hall. The Bellevue House piano stood against the wall. Colin had not seen it as he came in, and the sight disturbed him. He could not work out boundaries anymore. Where did the fat man start and end? Bette sat at the piano, and Verna stood by her. There were not enough chairs for everyone else.

"You and me can sit on the stairs, Laurie, eh? You, too, kid."

But Colin stood by his mother's chair. He could not protect his father but thought he might save her. Bette sang three songs in her thin voice—it seemed more fragile now, more broken at the edges. Light from the stained-glass window streamed down on the fat man, turning his skull red and green. He smiled at everyone with pointed teeth, disturbing the worm in his cheek.

"I love good music. It does something to me deep inside. Let's have 'Old-Fashioned Mother' to finish up."

Bette sang. Colin saw a tear gleam high on her cheek, but knew it was for herself, and maybe Verna, too, not for the words. It made a path through her powder, showing a dark line of bruise underneath.

How well I remember in years long gone by,
Together we sat, she and I,
More like two old sweethearts than mother and son,
In days long since gone with a sigh . . .

"Aah," said the fat man when it was over, "that was good. That was for my mum. God bless you, Mum. Now we can all have a beer. In the kitchen, that's the place for beer."

So they trooped there. The fat man was marshaling them like sheep. Only Grandma Potter had the spirit to fight back.

"I don't like beer-drinking when children are around."

"Doesn't do them any harm. Let them have one, too," the fat man said.

"Over my dead body."

The fat man gave her an ugly look, but Grandma ignored it. "Outside, children. Go and play."

Colin was so eager to escape, he wasn't offended by her treating him as a child. He and Verna went into the yard. For a while they looked at the half-built shed, then they went further, to the creek.

"Did they ever get her hat?" Colin asked.

"Someone did. He burned it. He burned all her old clothes."

"But he hugs her pillow?"

"He cries in it, too. I saw him in there once sucking his thumb."

Colin was terrified. "He'd have killed you if he'd seen."

"I suppose she was the only one who ever loved him."

"How do you think he feels now, drowning her?"

"I don't know, but I don't think he just pretends to cry."

They looked at the pool where Mrs. Muskie had drowned. Somewhere at the bottom were her jewels. Colin wished his father's boxing cups were down there, too.

"Show me where you met him," Verna said.

"It's half an hour."

"I don't care."

They went down the bank and along the side of the creek in the shade. Colin took off his shoes to cross the half-sunken log. He carried them stuffed into his shirt. They climbed along the hanging roots and crossed back on the stones.

"There's the bridge."

Black moss grew on its underside. It made them feel bent and small and out of the world.

"He says he helped kill people in Detroit."

"How?" Verna whispered.

"He sank them through the ice."

The blackberries had grown. Colin put his shoes on and picked his way through. Verna followed, keeping close.

"That's the pool I saw him in. He was washing himself."

"With nothing on?"

"Yeah. Like a whale." They laughed. But there was no controlling the fat man in that way. "The hut's up here."

Autumn and winter had rotted it. Spiders had built their nests, and somewhere under the roof there would be wetas.

"It was a good hut once. We could have come here."

Verna shivered. "Not now."

"No, not now."

"We should go back."

"There's a better pool down a bit. We can sit in the sun."

They walked another minute or two and came to a wide pool lit on half its surface by the sun.

"We could swim here if it was summer," Colin said.

"I never want to swim in this creek."

They sat on the bank. "Mum and me are going to run away," Verna said.

"I thought you said he'd find you?"

"Not if we go far enough. Sometimes he goes away all night and all the next day. Next time he does that, we're going to get a taxi and go to Auckland. Then we'll get the train to Wellington. Mum's saving up."

"But I won't see you."

"I know. But he says he's going to kick Mum out and keep only me. He's going to get a new woman, he says."

"Who?"

"He won't tell her. He says he's got one sorted out,

but he's got to get rid of the husband first."

Colin knew. He could hardly breathe.

"I think he's talking about your mum and dad."

"Yes."

"What will you do?"

"Tell them. I've got to tell them everything."

"Is he like this just because your dad bullied him at school?"

"I don't know."

"And your mum used to laugh at him?"

"I don't know."

"How can we make someone believe us?"

She told him about her life: how her mother and father used to work on the stage, Bette and Howard Barrowclough. They traveled around singing at concerts and private parties. Her father juggled, too, and did conjuring tricks, and he often toured primary schools, calling himself Doctor Chuckles.

"He came to our school, when I was in the primers," Colin cried. "He balanced lots of chairs on his nose."

"That was his best trick. Mum couldn't travel much after she had me. But my dad and her were always laughing. Dad used to throw me up and catch me on one hand, like on a chair, and I'd sit right up by the ceiling. Then he used to drop me and catch me by the floor."

"What happened to him?"

"He got sick. He died. And Mum got poor. So she had to marry someone else."

"Him."

"Yes, him."

"Now he's after my mum and dad."

They sat in the sun, side by side. After a while Verna lay down.

"Are you going to sleep?"

"I can't sleep at night. I lie awake. I listen for him."

"I'll watch. I'll wake you up."

He looked at her sharp face as she slept. It seemed to soften as her breathing grew deeper. A blackbird was singing high on the far bank, in a tree fern. The sun moved off the surface of the pool. Shade crept up his legs, and Verna's, too, but his body stayed warm in the sun. Verna's hair shone. Her new-grown curls fell across her forehead. She's going away, he thought, and was glad if it made her safe. The late afternoon train whistled at the crossing, and he remembered how, on that first day, at the hut, another train had whistled and the fat man had asked him the time. Everything had changed on that day. He had changed. His mother and father had changed. It was like an open door, and the fat man had come through from the dark place where he lived.

Colin touched the curls on Verna's forehead. The blackbird stopped singing. He felt a thickening in the air behind him. He felt a coldness on his neck.

"I thought I might find you here," the fat man said softly.

Colin turned around. He shrank inside, but tried to keep from showing his fear.

"Verna's asleep."

"So I see. Like her, do you, eh, kid? Like her curls?" He stood in the half-shade at the top of the bank. Little round coins of sunlight lay on his face. He smiled and his teeth gleamed, wet with saliva. "Can't say I blame you. Pretty curls."

Verna was awake. Her eyes had opened once and then closed. Only her breathing had changed. It almost stopped.

"I reckon you're in love, kid."

"No," Colin said.

"Sure, don't pretend. Say it, eh."

"Not to you."

"Hey, kid, you're going to make me mad. And you can quit pretending, Vern. I know you're awake."

Verna sat up. "What do you want?"

"Nothing much. Just if the kid here loves you, eh?"

"Yes, he does. So leave us alone."

The fat man smiled. The worm made a sudden upward twist into the sun. "Well, ain't that peachy. Colin Potter loves Verna Muskie. If I had a knife with me, I'd carve it on a tree."

"We're not hurting anyone," Verna said.

"Never said you were. Hey, Vern, relax. I just come to find you. The party's all over back there. It's time we went home."

"Is Mum all right?"

"Sure she is. What would happen to her? Funny, women, aren't they, kid? They get ideas in their heads."

"Don't you touch us," Colin said.

"Hey, I'm not going to touch you. I'm just going to tidy things up a bit. Now both of you follow me or else I'll change me mind." He turned and started up the creek. Verna stood up, and she and Colin followed. They kept as far back as they dared.

"What's he going to do?" Colin whispered.

"I don't know."

They went under the bridge, crossed the log, climbed the bank. Bette stood in the kitchen door, with her hand shading her eyes from the last of the sun.

"Oh, Verna," she cried, "where have you been? I've been so worried."

"Shut up, Bette. She's all right. Go and finish the dishes," the fat man said.

"Verna—"

"Did you hear me or didn't you?"

"Yes, I'm sorry." Bette turned back inside and was busy at the sink when Colin and Verna came in. She had a pile of dirty plates beside her.

"I'll help, Mum," Verna said.

"No, you won't." The fat man pulled a chair out from the table. "You sit there. And don't you move. Stay where you are, kid." He went out and climbed the stairs.

"Oh, Verna, I told you not to upset him," Bette trembled.

"I didn't. We just went down the creek."

They heard the fat man upstairs, walking in the bedroom. In a moment he came down whistling a tune—"Three Little Words."

"Well, Vern, here we go," he said.

"What . . ."

"We're going to give you a haircut." He took his razor out of his pocket and opened the blade.

Bette started from the bench, crying, "No!" but the fat man turned on her, quick as a cat. His good humor was gone. "Keep away," he snarled. Bette sank to the floor by the stove and covered her mouth. Verna could not move from the chair. Her face, usually pale, had gone even whiter. Colin took a step toward her.

"You, too, kid. Keep away." Then, like switching stations on the radio, he smiled. It terrified Colin. It seemed he could change into anything.

"All I'm doing," the fat man said, "is trimming up me daughter. Sit still, Vern. Don't want to nick you." He lifted a curl from her forehead and sliced it neatly off with the razor.

"Here you are, kid. Like to keep it for a souvenir?"

"No," Colin whispered.

"Suit yourself." He dropped it on the floor. Then, curl by curl, sometimes gentle, sometimes with a slash, he cut Verna's hair, until it lay jagged, half an inch long, all over her head. He sighed when it was done, and smiled at Bette still crumpled by the stove. "Take a look, Bette. Good job, eh?"

"Yes," Bette wept into her hands.

"Look, I said." He was snarling again, and Bette took her hands away and looked at Verna blindly.

"Yes. Yes."

"Think she's pretty?"

"Yes, she's pretty."

"You're lying, Bette. What I've done is make her ugly, see? Look at her. What is she, Bette?"

"She—she's ugly."

"Yeah, that's right. And what about you, kid? Curls all gone. Do you still love her?"

Colin looked at Verna sitting in the chair with her eyes shrunken and her mouth wrung shut and a dead curl caught in the neck of her dress. Her hair was chopped off, but he knew that, yes, he loved her even more than before. In spite of that, he knew what he must say.

"No, not now."

The fat man sighed. He sat down, closed his razor, and laid it on the table. "There, you see, Bette, saved her from a fate worse than death. Get me a beer, eh?"

Bette struggled up and took a bottle of beer from the cupboard. She opened it and put it in front of the fat man, with a glass.

"Thanks, sugar." He filled the glass and drank half of it in a gulp. "Leave the dishes. Come and sit on me knee." Then he saw Colin.

"You still here, kid? I'm gettin' a bit sick of the sight of you. Beat it, eh?"

Colin threw a last look at Verna in her chair. He went out of the kitchen and around the side of the house and ran home through the darkening streets.

CHAPTER 8

Flying Fox

Laurie was setting out to look for Colin when he saw him running up the street. He stood at the gate and waited. Laurie was unhappy at that time—he was unhappy with himself—and was close to taking it out on Colin.

"Where've you been?"

Colin ran by him. He ran up the path, through the kitchen, into the bedroom, into a corner. Then there was no place to go. His mother and father crowded in the door.

"Colin, what's wrong?"

"He cut her hair."

"Who? What are you talking about?"

"Herbert Muskie cut Verna's hair. With his razor." A strange thing—Colin called him Herbert Muskie from this time, as though they had moved closer and the fat man had a name.

He sat on his bed and cried. His mother came and put her arms around him.

"Colin? Colin?"

"Herbert Muskie cut Verna's hair."

"Why?"

"He's cut it off the way it was before."

"He's upset, Colin. Because of his mother."

"He's going to get us all," Colin cried. "He's getting even."

"That's enough," Laurie said. "It must have been a joke. Herbie's got a funny sense of humor."

"Dad . . ."

"Or maybe he thought she needed it. Verna's a bit too uppity. She's full of herself."

Colin could not believe it. There was no one now who would understand.

"And I've just about had enough from you," Laurie said. "I want my tea, Maisie. I'm going out."

"Where?"

"With Herbie. Into Auckland. He wants me to help him move some stuff."

"Laurie—"

"He's giving me a fiver. It's money." He went to the door, turned back, found nothing to say. How unhappy with himself Laurie was. "So let's have tea."

He left the room, and Maisie sat with Colin for a moment.

"Don't upset your father, son. I don't like Herbie much, either. But we'll be finished with him soon. Your dad will find a carpentry job."

"Mum . . ." He could not explain.

"I know how much you like Verna. It'll grow again."

"Don't let him go with Herbert Muskie."

Maisie stood up. "Now I've had enough, too. You're letting your imagination run away with you."

"Please, Mum."

"You needn't come out for tea. We don't want you when you're like this."

Maisie went out and closed the door. Colin felt as if he'd lost his parents. Herbert Muskie had them and was shifting them somewhere. He lay on his bed. He tried to think of something to do. Muskie was moving faster now. He was mad and clever, mad and sane; he slipped in and out. If Colin had not said that he did not like Verna anymore, he might have killed her with his razor. What would he do to Laurie? Something much cleverer than that. Herbert Muskie would stay sane for that.

He heard his mother serving tea, but did not go out. Lying in the dark, he heard them talking. Laurie even laughed once. It was a dreadful sound. Maisie washed the dishes. The dishes made a dreadful sound, too. He wondered if Bette had got off Herbert Muskie's knee and gone back to her own dishes. He wondered if Verna was still in her chair, staring at the wall.

A car came up the road. He knew the engine noise. It stopped at the gate and the horn honked, da-da-dee-da-da. Herbert Muskie played his tune.

Colin heard his father leave the house. He heard him walk down the path and could have leaned out and touched his hair. The car door opened. Herbert Muskie laughed. The door slammed. Colin heard the car move away and the engine noise grow fainter. It swelled a little, going up the hill to the Great North Road, then died out. His father was gone.

After a while his mother opened the door.

"Are you awake, Colin?"

"Yes."

"Come and have your tea." Her voice was kind, but seemed to him very far away. He got up and went into the kitchen. She took his plate from the oven and put it in front of him: doughboy and stew. "Your favorite." He tried to eat. More oranges from Herbert Muskie were sitting in a bowl in the middle of the table. He put some stew in his mouth, but could not swallow it.

"It's too much of that cake," his mother said crossly. "You'd better clean your teeth and go to bed."

He took a lighted candle up the path, used the lavatory, and sat there for a while. Spiders had crawled out on the ceiling, and the light gleamed on their coal-black heads. Colin was frightened of them, but more frightened of Herbert Muskie, although he knew he would fight him now, he would bite and kick. But nothing of that mattered because he was too late.

"Colin, hurry up. Don't sit there," his mother called.

He washed, he brushed his teeth, he went to bed, and must have been exhausted because he went to sleep—and when he woke, everything changed, he was able to talk and act and do things at last. He woke with his mother sitting on his bed.

"Colin," she said, "it's two o'clock."

"Did Dad come home?"

"No, he's still out. Colin, I'm worried."

"Herbert Muskie's got him. He's getting even."

"What for?"

"For Dad bullying him at school. And you laughing at him."

"But that was years ago," Maisie said. "What's he doing, Colin? What's he doing?"

"He's been after us ever since he came."

He told his mother everything—the pool, the hut, the chocolate; and Mrs. Muskie's sovereigns, and taking the fat man's shilling—although he called him Herbert Muskie now.

"I was his accomplice," Colin said, "so I couldn't tell you. I'm sorry, Mum. I didn't know till later on he was after Dad."

"And me?"

"Verna says you. Mum, he drowned his mother. He drowned Mrs. Muskie."

"No. No. He loved her too much."

"That doesn't matter."

"You saw him crying."

"He cried for her, but he killed her, too."

"Oh, oh," Maisie wept.

"And he brought you oranges. That was getting you."

"Oh, oh."

"Don't cry, Mum."

"Where's your father? Where's he gone?"

They sat in the kitchen waiting. They tried to think of things to do—go to the Muskies' house, call the police—but nothing would help until they found out what had happened to Laurie.

In the dark hours, well before dawn, they heard feet on the path. Laurie panted at the door. He opened it and almost fell inside.

"Laurie," Maisie screamed.

"I walked and ran," he panted. "All the way from Auckland. I walked and ran."

"Laurie, what happened? Are you all right?"

"I got away from him. I got away from Herbie."

"Laurie—"

"Has he come here? I thought he'd come here?"

"No one's come. Oh, Laurie, sit down. Thank God you're safe."

"He nearly got me, Maise. I got away."

They made him sit at the table. The stove was still warm. Maisie started it up and put water on for tea while Laurie told them what had happened in Auckland.

At first they'd gone to a friend of Herbert Muskie's and had a few beers. (It was the man who had bought Laurie's boxing cups, but Laurie did not know that. Nothing was said about cups on this occasion.) Then they'd driven to a shed in Grafton and started shifting stuff from it to another shed in Morningside.

"I didn't like it, Maise. It was all sorts of things. Radios and electric irons and stuff like that. Whiskey and tobacco. Cigarettes. There was even tins of salmon. Rounds of cheese. I started wondering if it was stolen. I asked Herbie what it was, but all he said was that it was Ron's. Ron's the other bloke, where we had the drink. Herbie says he's got a shop and this was discount stuff he'd bought, and fire sale stuff. So I—just went along with it, Maise. I didn't want to make a fool of myself."

They made half a dozen trips, with the car packed full. Then Herbert Muskie asked Laurie to drive.

"He told me he might give me a job making deliveries, so I better start driving straight away. For practice, he said. It's a good car, Maise. It's great to drive."

"Oh, Laurie."

"Yeah, I know. But I didn't see what he was up to then. I just sort of got in and drove, out to Remuera, all the way. Herbie said he had a man to see. I thought that was funny. It was after midnight."

They parked in the dark part of a street, and Herbert Muskie told Laurie to wait. He got out and walked back up the road, fifty yards.

"He was carrying this kind of roll. It was made of canvas. It looked like a tool kit, you know, small."

"He's a burglar," Colin said.

"Be quiet, Colin. Go on, Laurie."

"He went into a house—well, he went in the gate—and I waited a bit. I didn't like it. I got out and rolled myself a smoke. Then I heard glass break. It was real soft. I hardly heard. So I walked back up the road to the house where Herbie was. There were no lights, Maise."

"He's a burglar."

"Colin!"

"So I looked in at the gate and then I saw him. It was a big house, two-stories, and he was upstairs. I knew it was him by his shadow. He must have been using a torch and he'd put it down somewhere and it shone on him a minute and made this shadow on the wall. His hat. His gut. I knew straight away what he was doing. God, how could I be so dumb?"

"What did you do?"

"I got out the gate. I took off. At first I was going to take the car, but then I just ran. I ran and walked all the way home. Too late for the buses. It took me four hours, Maise. A couple of cars passed me, but I thought it might be Herbie so I hid."

"You should have gone straight to the police."

"I will. Tomorrow. But I had to get back here. I thought he might come here. Maise, while I was walking I worked it all out. He was trying to turn me into a crook."

"You'd be his accomplice," Colin said. "He'd have got you, then."

"Yeah, I guess."

"And when you went to prison he'd come and get Mum."

"Colin," Maisie said, "tell your father what you told me."

Colin told it again, from the time he had met Herbert Muskie at the creek right up to him cutting Verna's hair—and everything was plain to see in the story now, except that, just like Maisie, Laurie could not believe Herbert Muskie had drowned his mother.

"He's been after everyone," Colin said. "His brother and his sisters. But mainly you and Mum."

"But his mother. He loved her."

"She couldn't save him, though. When he was a boy."

He saw Herbert Muskie's madness clearer than the others. He saw how it could swing from murder, and open cruelty, like Verna's hair, to the cleverness of sucking Laurie in and waiting for Maisie.

"You should have told us about the sovereigns, Colin. Then none of this might have happened."

"Laurie, you mustn't blame him."

"I was his accomplice," Colin said. "He got me caught."

"He nearly got me," Laurie said. "As soon as it's light, I'm going to see Bill Dreaver."

But the darkness seemed to go on and on.

"What if Herbert Muskie comes here?" Colin said.

Laurie went to the washhouse and got his hammer. He laid it on the table. "I'll be ready," he said.

"What about Verna, though? What about her?"

"She'll be all right, son. And Bette. They haven't hurt him," Maisie said.

"We should go 'round and tell them. So they can get away."

"No," Laurie said. "Leave it to the police. They can handle it. I'll tell them about that shed in Morningside."

Meanwhile, the fat man—or Herbert Muskie, as we must call him now—had worked out that Laurie would do that. When he came out of the Remuera house and found him gone, he drove around searching in the streets. He even drove halfway to Loomis and would have gone all the way and waited close to Laurie's house, but the danger of Laurie going straight to the police was too great. He had to shift the goods in the shed, make them safe. Then he could do something about Laurie Potter. He could not take the slow revenge he had wanted. He would have to make him vanish, kill him quick.

He woke the man called Ron and they worked fast.

They shifted the goods from the Morningside shed to a garage in Kingsland, close by. Even so, it took longer. Ron was not as fit and strong as Laurie. Herbert Muskie left him at the garage and went for the last load by himself. But their luck had run out. All this shifting and driving before dawn had alerted a woman who lived close to the garage in Kingsland—she suffered from varicose veins, she said, they kept her awake at night with their aching—and she sent her husband out the back door and over the garden fence to fetch the police.

As Herbert Muskie was driving back, he saw a police car turn into the street where the garage was. He made a U-turn and drove away. He headed for Loomis. They would catch Ron and Ron would talk; he would try to save his skin by putting as much blame as he could on his partner. Herbert Muskie drove recklessly, and raged inside. He had to get away, tonight; he had to find a place to hide. Laurie and Maisie Potter—that must be put off. But when he was ready, he would come back.

Halfway up the Waikumete hill he stopped and dumped most of the goods in the cemetery pine forest. He kept a bottle of whiskey and some cigarettes. Dawn was breaking as he pulled up outside his house in Loomis. All he wanted here were his emergency money and a suitcase of spare clothes.

But where would he go? How would he hide? His size, his scar, made it almost impossible.

A hostage, Herbert Muskie thought. I need a hostage.

He let himself into the house and went upstairs

quietly. Quietly he opened Verna's door.

She was not there. Her bed was empty, not even slept in.

Herbert Muskie ran to Bette's room—and there Verna was, with her cropped hair, sharing the double bed with her mother. Two white faces looked over the eiderdown at him.

"Get up, Vern, and get your clothes on quick. You're coming with me."

"No," Bette cried. "You're not taking her."

Verna scrambled out of bed and tried to duck past Muskie in the door. She meant to get out of the house and run somewhere—anywhere.

Herbert Muskie caught her arm. He shook her. He cuffed her. "Shut up," he said. "And you, too," he said to Bette in the bed.

But Bette jumped out and tried to attack Herbert Muskie. He threw her away one-handed. "The cops are after me. You'll get her back when I'm safe, not before." He took the key from the lock, stepped out, and locked the door, dragging Verna by the arm.

"Now you," he said, "get some clothes. Not too many. And stop your sniveling, it's getting on me nerves."

He pushed her into her bedroom and watched while she tried to gather clothes from a drawer. He had forgotten Bette. He thought that she was useless. But now Bette was driven by her love for Verna, and perhaps her love for her dead husband, too. People were starting to act against Herbert Muskie at last.

Bette climbed out her bedroom window. Laurie had not taken down his scaffolding yet. She climbed to the ground. Then she ran out the front gate and along the road, in her nightie, bruising her feet on the metal. She ran for the only place she could think of. Maisie and Laurie and Colin, eating breakfast early, heard her feet on the path; a pattering like dead leaves in a storm.

"Maisie," she sobbed as they opened the door, "he's taking Verna with him. He's running away."

Colin took off without a word. He was out the door before anyone could stop him. He knew his father would follow on his bike, and his mother would get the police. He had to reach Verna before she was gone. He had to stop Herbert Muskie taking her away. Poor Colin. A seven-stone boy, a quiet, gentle boy, cannot fight an eighteen-stone man with murder on his mind. It's just as well he did not have to face Herbert Muskie alone. Laurie caught him outside the gate to the Muskie house. Laurie had left fast, too, but getting his bike from the shed had taken time. He had forgotten his hammer.

The Buick stood outside the gate. A tangle of Verna's clothes lay on the back seat, with a suitcase, initialed H.J.M., four-square beside it. Herbert Muskie was a tidy man. Two brown-paper bags stained with grease filled the rest of the seat.

"Stay here, Colin," Laurie said, but Colin disobeyed him and followed up the path. They were halfway to the front door when a bursting sound, a shattering, came from the side of the house and something heavy crashed into the hydrangeas.

So many things were taking place, it's difficult to remember them all. We must go back a step or two and say what happened to Verna.

Herbert Muskie never let her get more than an arm's length away. She gathered her clothes, an armful, haphazardly, then waited while he packed his suitcase in his mother's bedroom, where he kept his clothes in the dressing table and the wardrobe. He took her to the bathroom and locked her in with him while he washed and shaved. She watched as he lathered his face and stropped his razor. If he hadn't had a pee in the pine trees at Waikumete, she might have had to go to the toilet and watch that, too. Then they went back to his mother's bedroom and he put on clean underclothes and a shirt and suit and tie. For a moment he was half-naked in the room. Verna hid her eyes.

They took their clothes out to the car and put them on the backseat. "Food," Herbert Muskie said. They returned to the house and he made her fill paper bags with the cakes and sandwiches left over from the party. They took them out, too. (He had already got his money. The hiding place was the chamber pot in his mother's commode.)

"Get in," he said, and Verna climbed into the passenger seat. She was trying to be careful and do everything he said. She was so frightened of him that even if he gave her the chance to run, her legs would not have carried her far. He stood at the driver's door and looked at the house. He must have known he would never come back to it.

"No," he said, "get out."

He did not wait for her to move but opened the door and reached across and dragged her past the steering wheel. He slammed the door and they went back to the house. Verna was sure he was taking her there to kill her. Her legs stopped working. Herbert Muskie jerked her up and swore, then carried her the rest of the way under his arm. He went inside and closed the front door, and at that moment Colin ran into Millbrook Road. He missed by a whisker seeing them go in.

Herbert Muskie went through the entrance hall into the kitchen. He swung Verna onto the table and sat her there. "Don't move." He went to a cupboard, straight to what he wanted, his mother's old stone rolling pin, as heavy as the axle of a car.

"Come with me."

Verna could not move. He pulled her off the table, stood her up. "Walk, girl. I'm not carrying you." He pushed her once, twice, to the entrance hall. "Stand there."

Then Herbert Muskie lined up the stained-glass window. He swung the rolling pin in a round-arm loop to judge its weight. Verna felt the wind of it on her face. He set himself, held still for a moment, then threw it with an easy motion, overarm. It flipped twice in the air, like a thrown knife, hit the window in its center, burst it into pieces, and fell into the hydrangeas outside. That was the noise Colin and Laurie heard from the front path.

"Stay here. I mean it," Laurie cried. He ran around the side of the house. As he went from sight the front door opened and Herbert Muskie appeared, holding

Verna by the hand like a man taking his daughter to school.

"So, it's the kid," Herbert Muskie said. He ran at Colin, pounced at him before he could move, dragging Verna all the way. He caught him with his free hand at the nape of his neck.

"Gotcha, kid,"

Colin yelled and tried to fight, but Herbert Muskie tightened his fingers and held him still. "Now I got two hostages," he said.

Laurie came back around the side of the house. He had found the rolling pin. He saw Herbert Muskie and started at him, but Muskie saw him, too, and yelled, "Stay back, Pottsie. I'll wring your kid's neck if you move."

His fingers bit. Laurie saw Colin's anguished face. He stopped his advance.

"Let him go, Herbie. Then I'll let you go."

Herbert Muskie laughed. "Ah, Pottsie, don't be a sap. I got the aces." He shook Colin, he shook Verna. He had switched his grip on her and had her, too, by the nape of the neck. "Now chuck away your waddy. Over the fence back there. Chuck it! I'll bang their heads together, you reckon I won't?"

Laurie measured the distance between them and saw he had no choice. He threw the rolling pin over the fence into the bushes.

"Let them go now, Herbie. They haven't done any-thing to you."

"Ah, Pottsie, that's not the point. I need them 'cause the cops are after me. Now you stay where you are and I won't hurt them. It only needs a little squeeze. Tell 'im, kid."

"Dad," Colin managed to say.

"It's all right, Colin. I'm not going to do anything."

"Pleased to hear it," Herbert Muskie said. He backed away several steps, walking Colin and Verna, then turned and pushed them ahead of him as far as the gate. "Open it."

Verna lifted the catch and pulled it open. She did not seem as tightly held as Colin. Herbert Muskie walked them to the car. "Back door." She opened it. "In you go." He pushed her in across the bags of food. Then he took Colin in two hands and threw him on top of her and slammed the door.

Laurie saw his chance. He ran across the weedy lawn and took the picket fence like a hurdler. Herbert Muskie, halfway into the driver's seat, heard him coming. He backed out and spun around, with his freakish quickness, and stepped toward Laurie, two steps. Laurie forgot his boxing. His run took him in close. He sprang at Herbert Muskie, who bellowed and wrapped him in two arms. His shoulders bulged, his face turned red, as he gave a squeeze. Laurie dropped broken on the ground. Muskie would have trampled on him then, or strangled him, but a car turned off the bridge into Millbrook Road.

Colin, untangling himself from Verna in the backseat, saw it from the rear window. Herbert Muskie saw it, too, and recognized it—a police car. He moved a step at Laurie, then moved away, flung a look of hatred at him— "I'll be back for you, Pottsie"—and scrambled into the car. He got it started, roared away, slamming through the gears, before Colin and Verna could climb out.

How did the police car get there? It was just as Herbert Muskie had supposed. Ron tried to put the blame on his partner. He told the police all about Herbert Muskie and that he lived in Loomis, although Ron didn't know where. The Auckland detectives telephoned Constable Dreaver, who was waiting for them when they arrived at his station. He got into the car and they drove to Millbrook Road and were just in time to save Laurie's life. They might have caught Herbert Muskie if they hadn't stopped to see if the man lying at the side of the road was all right. Dreaver stayed with him—Laurie had two cracked ribs—and the detectives took off again after Muskie's car, but by that time he was more than a mile ahead. The dust had died down. They came to a fork in the road and took the wrong turning.

So Herbert Muskie got away with his two hostages. By nine o'clock that morning every policeman in Auckland was keeping an eye out for a green Buick sedan, driven by a fat man with a scar on his cheek, and two children, a boy and a girl, riding with him. But the car was clear by that time. Herbert Muskie had circled back to Auckland and driven through the southern suburbs of the city. He took back roads through farming country and reached the sea on the Hauraki Gulf. He drove along the coast road at an even pace and even whistled once—whistled "Alabamy Bound."

Colin and Verna sat huddled on the backseat. They had made a place for themselves among Verna's clothes. Several times, on corners where the car had to slow down, they wondered if there would be a chance to open the door and jump out. They did not try to get the attention of the few people they passed. Herbert Muskie had said, while in the suburbs, "If you wave or squeal, you two back there, you're goners. Understand?" They understood. Colin tried to think of plans; Verna, too. He thought he might lean over Herbert Muskie's shoulder and grab the wheel and steer the car into a ditch. She thought she might get a handful of mashed-up cake from the paper bag and smear it in Herbert Muskie's eyes. That would give them a chance. . . .

Neither of them did anything. They didn't talk, even in whispers. They held hands. Colin looked at her from time to time to see if she was still all right. Her hair was jaggedly cut all over her head. A speck of dried blood showed where the razor had nicked her. Apart from that she looked the way she had on her first morning at Loomis school. She even wore the same dress.

Once she whispered to him, "Is your neck all right?"

"Yes," he nodded, although nodding hurt. Herbert Muskie's fingers had dug deep.

At ten o'clock Muskie stopped the car in a side road by a muddy beach.

"Hand me some of that chocolate sponge."

Verna found a piece in the bag and passed it to him.

"You squash this on purpose, Vern?"

"No."

Herbert Muskie ate. "You, kid. There's a bottle of whiskey there, beside me case."

Colin passed it over, and Muskie swigged a mouthful. "You two can eat. Go on."

"No thank you," Verna said.

"I'm not hungry," Colin said.

"Suit yourselves. Did you see what I did to your old man, kid?"

"He's all right. The police were helping him sit up."

"Too bad." He opened the glove box and took out a ball of twine. "Get out of the car." He was out himself, with his usual quickness, by the time they opened the door.

"Are you going to tie us up?" Verna said.

"I want you in the front with me. I don't like people behind. The kid here's dumb enough to try something. You thought you might hit me with me whiskey, eh, kid?"

"No," Colin said.

"Sure you did. I don't mind. I like a kid with guts. And when you get in front, eh, you might try grabbing the wheel. So . . ." He took out his pocketknife and cut a length of twine.

"I need to go to the lavatory," Verna said.

"He'll close his eyes," Herbert Muskie joked, but he let her go alone into the bushes. "I don't reckon you're gonna run while I still got the kid."

When she came back, Colin went. Then Herbert Muskie tied them together, Verna's right wrist to Colin's right, so Colin, sitting beside him, would have his arm across his waist. He took a can of petrol from the boot and poured it into the tank. Before leaving, he peed, too, at the back of the car. Then they drove on, through Ngatea and across the top of the Hauraki Plains—although Colin and Verna did not know these names and Herbert Muskie wasn't too familiar with them. He was just putting distance between himself and Loomis.

As they drove he lost his good humor. They climbed hills and wound through gorges. "Bloody roads, they should make 'em straight."

"Where are we going?" Colin said.

"Belt up, kid. You don't need to know."

"You can't get away."

"Lippy, eh? Like your old man. You sure he was moving?"

"Yes."

"So I guess we're not even. How's he gonna like losing you?"

Verna jerked Colin's arm to make him be quiet.

They drove along hillsides, high above rivers that turned from green to white among the rocks. At one o'clock Herbert Muskie pulled into a clay road that angled off behind a clump of trees. "Out," he said.

They climbed out awkwardly, tied together. Scrubby hills, eroded with slips, fell away to the distant coast. A cold wind was blowing, and clouds were piling up on the higher hills behind them.

"Can you untie us?" Verna asked.

"No."

"I want to put on something warmer."

"No, I said. Bring out them sandwiches. Leave the cake."

"We need a drink."

"There's a creek over there. Don't try and run."

They went across a paddock close-cropped by sheep and knelt at the edge of a shallow pool. They drank with their faces at the water.

"Now we could run."

"No, we couldn't."

"Yeah, we need to be untied."

"What's he going to do with us, do you think?"

"Keep us until he's safe."

"What then?"

They went back to the car. Herbert Muskie was eating ham sandwiches, taking them from the bag in threes. He had a swig of whiskey from his bottle.

"Can I have a sandwich?" Verna asked.

"Thought you weren't hungry."

"I am now." She took two sandwiches from the bag and gave one to Colin. They sat on the sheltered side of the car and ate. Herbert Muskie put the bottle inside. He came around and sat with them, holding the paper bag.

"Sandwiches, eh? Did I tell you, kid, what Pottsie and his mates used to do to me at Loomis school? They'd come lookin' for me at lunchtime and they'd get all around me friendly like, and Pottsie would say, 'We've got a sandwich for you, Herbie.' One of them would hold it out, and then they'd pull it back and say, 'We'll just make it taste better, eh?' They'd take the top off, see, like this." He took the last sandwich from the bag and lifted the top off, showing the ham. "Then they'd all spit on it, each one. Four or five of them, like this." He did not spit on the ham but out to one side. "Then they'd put it back together again and make me eat it. Spit sandwich was its name. I ate one of those every day."

Colin knew that this was not a lie. He felt his father shrink to something small and dark inside him. "Why didn't you tell someone?" he whispered.

"I never was a stoolie, kid." He threw the sandwich away.

"My mum didn't know."

"Sure she knew. The girls all knew. Pottsie and Poultice, eh? I been thinkin' about them for a good long time." He reached into the car and got his bottle. "I'd get into me bathing suit down at Cascade Park. We had to go for swimming, from school. The girls would be standin' 'round when I came out of the shed."

"What did they do?"

"Nothin' much, kid. They only laughed. Nothin' much."

He walked away and stood on a rise, looking down at the coast, drinking from the bottle.

"We've got to run," Verna said.

"My dad must have done it. What he said."

"It doesn't matter now. He's got his razor in his case. If we can get it out, we can cut this string."

She made him stand up, but Herbert Muskie turned. "Come here, you two. Hurry up."

They went up the slope to him. "What's he going to do?"

He pulled them roughly in front of him. "Look down there. What's that there, on that bit of road by the house?"

They looked where he pointed, far off, where a stretch

of road curved past the front of a farmhouse.

"A car," Verna said.

"With someone standing by it?"

"Two men."

"What I thought. It's a bloody roadblock, that's all."

"Is it the police?" Verna asked.

"Sure it is. And that means there's more of them coming up behind." He swore, using words Colin had only heard from the Rice gang before. And, of course, Herbert Muskie was right, there were more police coming behind. Someone had seen the Buick as it sped through a town, and reported it, and now Herbert Muskie was boxed in. He knew it and he swore again, and would have hurled his bottle at the roadblock, miles away, but held it back and had another drink.

"No one's lockin' me in any prison. Get back in the car. Go on, move it."

They ran, tied together, and climbed in. Herbert Muskie started the engine. "We're going up there."

"But it's only clay. It's only for horses."

"You frightened, kid? I thought you were the tough guy."

"No—"

"The bloke that pinches the chocolate, eh?"

"A car can't go up there."

"You wanna bet?" He drove the Buick, heaving, slow, like a farm tractor. It crossed and recrossed the creek, up to its running board in the water, then went up a bare hill, on a track worn by horses and sheep. Yellow clay broke under the wheels, and clods bounced down into the gully. Far off, the sea glittered and white beaches showed in bites of land. They saw the roadblock from time to time. Sunlight was mirrored from the windscreen of the car. If we can see them, they can see us, Colin thought. The Buick must be like a beetle crawling on the hill. Herbert Muskie had the same idea. The track went into a patch of bush. "We'll wait here," he said. "When they've gone, we'll drive down and head back the way we came. That'll fool them."

"You can't turn," Colin said. "There isn't any room."

"Don't get lippy, kid. I'll back down." But the heavy car, on the track, backing down the hill—it was impossible, he knew.

"There might be a turning place further up," Colin said.

"Shut up. I'm thinkin'."

Colin saw that he had lost his judgment, lost his way.

"Yeah, we'll wait here. There's no way they can find us here. Where's me whiskey?" He reached across to the glove box in front of Verna, where he had put it.

"The top's come off. It's all gone," Verna said.

"You do that, Vern? By God—"

"No, I didn't, it must have been the bumping. You didn't put the top on properly." Whiskey dripped from the glove box onto the floor.

"Jeez. No more bloody whiskey. I'm watchin' you kids from now on. If one of you steps out of line—"

"Hadn't we better look back down the track?" Colin said. He wanted to keep Herbert Muskie busy. If he talked and brooded, he would get dangerous.

"You think you're running this show, do you, kid?"

"No, but we might see the rest of them drive past."

Herbert Muskie lit a cigarette and dragged on it. "Okay. You're pretty smart. Out you get. No funny stuff."

The wind was less strong in the trees, but still blew cold. Gray clouds, piling up, moved across the sun. The land went darker suddenly and when they came to the edge of the bush, the hill looked different from the one they had driven up. They saw the place where they had stopped for lunch—a paddock hidden from the road, a ribbon of dark water. A little further off, toward the coast, a stretch of highway showed, running flat in a valley.

"There's a car."

"Ha, they've passed us. What did I say, kid?"

"There's another one coming the other way."

The cars met in the road and stopped, and the drivers talked from window to window.

"It's the one from the roadblock. They must have seen us."

"Shut up, kid. Let me think."

"The first one's turning 'round. They're coming back. Both of them."

Distantly they heard the cars racing on the road.

"They could go past. There's no way they can know where we turned off."

But in a moment the cars turned into the paddock and stopped close together. Three men got out of one and two from the other.

"Cops," Herbert Muskie breathed.

"They've found something. Your sandwich."

THE FAT MAN • • • • • • • • **175**

"They've found your tire tracks. They're looking up here."

"Back. Get back!" Muskie said. He heaved them out of sight.

"You can't get away now."

"I'm all right as long as I got you."

He made them run to the car and get in the front seat. They started off again, bucking and heaving in the ruts. The track climbed out of the bush, crossed a shallow ford, made a right-angle turn, and ran along the side of a new hill. A mile away, across a gully, they saw the two police cars climbing up. The back one stopped, and a man got out and waved his arms at them.

"If they think I'm givin' up, they're bloody mad," Herbert Muskie said. Then the track ran out. It petered into a watercourse that angled up the hill, from where distant sheep looked down from ledges. Herbert Muskie tried to drive on the grass and bracken.

"We're going to tip over," Verna said.

But the car stuck. Its chassis jammed on a hump, and the wheels, racing in reverse, would not pull it free.

"Out!" Muskie cried.

"We can't—"

"Out, I said. Jesus, kid, you want me to bash you?" He grabbed his suitcase from the backseat.

They ran on the hillside, heading toward a spur. Verna and Colin tripped and fell, but Herbert Muskie heaved them up and pushed them on. He crashed through bracken like a boar, then ran back at Colin and Verna and dragged and butted them through the track he had trampled. Sweat ran on his face. He had lost his hat. Oil from his hair greased his forehead and made it shine. He stopped for a moment and leaned and panted. With his case, he looked like a man who had missed his train.

Far away they heard men shouting. The front car had disappeared into the patch of bush, but the back one had stopped and the men from it had cut across the gully and were climbing the hill to head them off. Colin saw that they would be too late.

They ran again, and reached the spur. Another hillside, on a steeper plane, ran down to the edge of a gorge. Smooth rock walls dropped out of sight. Herbert Muskie roared with rage, roared like a bull. He looked around wildly, swinging his head. Then he roared again. This time it made a grieving sound.

"Wait for them here," Colin said.

"No. No." Something in him shifted and gave way. Herbert Muskie turned into the fat boy again, running from the playground gang at Loomis school.

"They're coming," he cried. "Where? Where?"— swinging his head for a place to hide. The scar in his cheek had almost gone, as though the worm had wriggled in and tried to get from sight.

"Give me the pocketknife," Colin said.

"He left it in the glove box," Verna said.

"Give me your case." He took it from Herbert Muskie's hand, opened the catches, found the razor, took it out. He cut the twine binding him and Verna. "Wait here," he said.

"Where are you going?"

"Not far. I don't think he can run much anymore."

It was true. Herbert Muskie was strong and quick, but he wasn't fit. He had reached the end of his strength, and of his knowledge of where he was.

"Do you want your case back?" Colin asked.

"Yes, me case. Gotta have me case. You helping me, Pottsie? You helping me now?"

"Where would you like to go? Down there?"

"Yes. They're coming. I can hear them. Down there."

They half-ran, half-walked, on the hillside, angling down toward the gorge. Verna watched them go, standing on the spur. The two nearest policemen were half a minute away, with the others not far behind. When she looked back at Colin and Herbert Muskie, they were at the edge of the gorge, walking along to the place where it bent from sight. She did not learn till later that a river ran down there.

Colin looked down at it. "We can't get across."

"Yes we can. We can climb."

"All we can do is go along here." He looked back. The two policemen ran into sight around the end of the spur. They stopped beside Verna, who pointed at the fat man.

"Muskie," one of them yelled. "Stop where you are."

"Let the boy go, Muskie."

"Come back, Colin," Verna called.

Instead, Colin ran. He ran with the fat man along the side of the gorge, listening to him pant and wheeze, seeing him stumble. He hoped the policemen would catch them soon.

"Look, Pottsie, there's a flying fox!"

The wire ran across the gorge to a post on the other side. It looked as thin as a cotton thread. Another post stood on the near side, with a bracing peg set in the ground. A wooden cage hung from a wheel. It was tied to the post, above a low platform made of planks.

The fat man stepped onto the platform. He put down his case and panted, hands on knees. "We can—cross. We can—get away."

"No," Colin said. "It'll break."

"You tellin' me what to do, kid?" Suddenly he was Herbert Muskie again, snarling at Colin. The worm twisted, fattened in his cheek.

Colin stepped back. He was safe. He could run.

"You're too heavy for it," he said.

Tears leaked from the fat man's eyes and dripped on the platform. He was changing back and forth. "Pottsie, you're helpin' me now. Aren't you, Pottsie?"

"If you want."

"Help me get in here, Pottsie. You and me are mates."

The policemen were running down the hill, yelling at them.

The fat man put his suitcase in the cage. He lifted one leg heavily and got it over the rail. The wire sagged with his weight, but he heaved the other leg in and squatted like a child in a box too small for it, holding the couplings with two hands. "They're comin', Pottsie. They're going to get me. Untie the rope."

Colin saw how eaten with rot the planks of the cage

were. It strained to get away down the wire. The river ran below, deep in the gorge, white and green.

"Please, Pottsie," Herbert Muskie wept.

Colin saw there was no way of untying the knot. The fat man's weight had pulled it too tight. He took the razor from his pocket and unfolded it.

"Do you want to go?"

"Yeah, Pottsie, cut it, eh. Go on, do it, kid."

Colin cut the rope. The wheel turned, it ran on the wire, and Colin heard the post creak as more weight came on. The cage moved out over the gorge, with the fat man in it. It rocked and surged, gaining speed.

When it reached the middle, the post broke. Colin heard a warning crack and jumped aside. Another crack, and the post slammed down across the platform, brushing his arm, breaking a bone there. He rolled off the platform and did not see Herbert Muskie fall.

Verna, running on the hillside, saw. The bracing peg held. The wire dropped ten feet, and the cage broke in pieces when it stopped.

Herbert Muskie fell. The fat man fell. He turned over once and struck the rocks at the side of the river and slid down them into the white water and was gone. His suitcase fell, too. It opened out its lid, and his shirts and underpants circled down like birds.

Verna ran to Colin, crying on the ground. She held him until policemen came to help.

CHAPTER 9

Later on . . .

Verna's hair grew again, and Colin's arm healed. But other things never came back to normal. Herbert Muskie's hand had been in too many things. The mill never reopened, for one thing, and Clyde became a drifter, almost a tramp, living on handouts from his posh sisters.

Grandpa Potter, as we know, went to prison for a month. He did not seem to mind it, or feel disgraced. In fact, he enjoyed playing the crooked old man, and when he came out he talked of reopening the sly-grog shop in the empty shed at the mill. Grandma soon put a stop to that. She locked him in one of the bedrooms at Bellevue House and would not let him out until he'd sworn on the Bible to go straight. Bellevue House never became a pub again, but as times improved, it did quite well as a boarding house.

When his broken ribs were healed, Laurie went back on relief. He never seemed to fully recover his spirits or his strength, although most people thought he had done well, standing up to Muskie at the end. He put his cups away in a cupboard. Maisie worked hard to cheer him up. He came off relief and worked as a carpenter until she persuaded him to go out on his own. Laurie began to prosper. He built most of the new shops in Loomis as the town grew and built a new house for Maisie, with a view over the harbor. She took out his cups again and polished them up and put them on the mantelpiece alongside the ones she was winning for croquet.

But let's get back to Colin and Verna.

His arm healed, her hair grew, as we've said. It would be nice to say that they grew up and married, but they only met once after the death of Herbert Muskie. Verna never went back to Loomis school. She stayed with her mother at Bellevue House for a week, then they shifted to Auckland and did not come to Loomis again.

Verna visited Colin before she left. They sat on the front steps in the sun, and she wrote her name in pencil on his plaster. (It soon got lost among the autographs he collected at school.)

"They all think I cut the rope because I was scared of him," Colin said.

He waved with his good hand as she went away.

For a while they wrote back and forth, a weekly exchange, then the letters stopped. But all through their lives they remembered each other.

Verna is the only one who knows why Colin ran with the fat man in the end, and cut the rope.